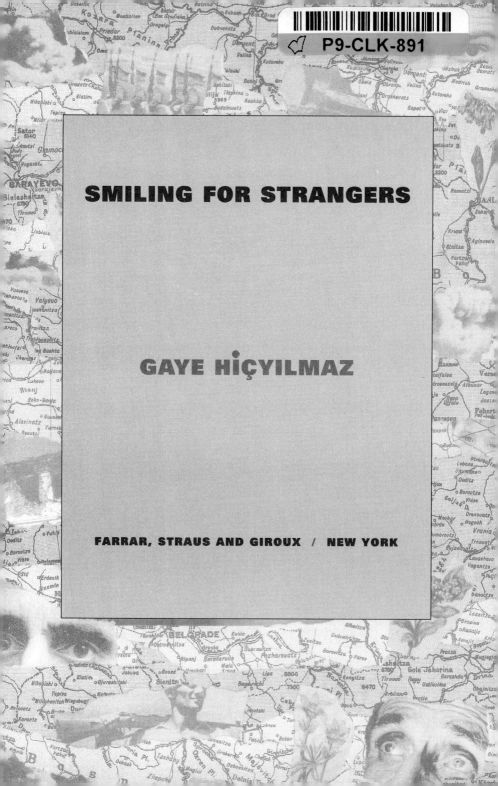

SMILING FOR STRANGERS

GAYE HİÇYILMAZ

FARRAR, STRAUS AND GIROUX / NEW YORK

Library of Congress Cataloging-in-Publication Data
Hiçyılmaz, Gaye.
    Smiling for strangers / Gaye Hiçyılmaz. — 1st American ed.
    p.   cm.
    Summary: During the war, fourteen-year-old Nina flees from her
village in Yugoslavia, armed only with some letters and a
photograph, to search for an old friend of her mother's in England.
    ISBN 0-374-37081-8
    1. Yugoslav War, 1991–1995—Juvenile fiction. [1. Yugoslav War,
1991–1995—Fiction. 2. Refugees—Fiction. 3. Yugoslavia—Fiction.]
I. Title.
PZ7.H53163Sm   2000
[Fic]—dc21   99-34508

FOR MY SISTER HEATHER,

without whose help

these books might not have been written

and certainly wouldn't have been typed

CONTENTS

SMILING FOR STRANGERS

1

WHERE WILD LAVENDER GREW

SOMEWHERE OUTSIDE, somewhere farther down the darkened track that led past their house, Nina could hear men's voices. Another group must be climbing toward the abandoned farms beyond. She was certain of this, not only because their voices were becoming louder, but because their progress was slow and irregular: they were struggling against the steepness of the hillside ascent. Those who returned from things done in the meadows and forests above always moved more quickly, as though the mountain were shaking them off.

In the morning, if she went outside, she would be able to see the prints left by their boots or running shoes: she would be able to tell where they had slipped in the deep mud and where they had crowded together, to discuss plans. The actions of these men were written into the landscape now. Once, during the thaw, she had seen three long-handled silver teaspoons dropped into the snow. They must have fallen from the hands or the pockets of one of the looters who had been scavenging in the farms on the higher slopes. She hadn't picked them up. She and her grandfather didn't need teaspoons and she had wondered what had made someone else take something so small. Maybe that was all that was left up there. Her grandfather had been up to look, but he hadn't let her come and he wouldn't tell her what he'd seen. He had been quiet afterward and insisted that she keep her bag packed, be ready to leave at any time.

Now he was snoring steadily on the other mattress. She was so used to it that she hardly noticed the sound, or only at times like this, when she was trying to concentrate and catch some other, different noise through its familiar rhythms. Her grandfather had always lived with her parents and Nina couldn't imagine life without him.

Years and years ago, when she had been a very little girl, her elder brothers used to tease her unmercifully. They always joked that her future husband would be a lucky fellow, because his wife would have grown up quite used to a man's snoring. She could remember one particular summer morning when both she and her grandfather, whose room she shared when the flat was crowded with visitors, had woken late. They had slept on into the thick heat of midday. Eventually she had scrambled, sticky and swollen-eyed, over the edge of the brass bed, where the old man still snored, and into the kitchen. Her older brothers and cousins sat around the table, smoking and stealing bits of food from the dishes which her mother and aunt were trying to assemble for some festive meal. How they had teased her!

The young men had grinned at her as she stomped toward them on the fat, flat feet of a four- or five-year-old. Now she was so thin that she couldn't believe that she had ever been that sturdy little girl whose round cheeks and plump wrists people had pinched and patted. On that lost summer morning, she had sidled toward Alexander's chair; the eldest of her brothers and fair-haired, he had always been her favorite. He had reached for her with one huge arm and drawn her toward him. She, irritable with too much sleep and the itch of new gnat bites on her shin, had pushed him away with all her sparrow's strength. He hadn't let her go, not even when she had put her little white teeth on the warm, sunburned skin of his forearm and bitten him. He hadn't even flinched. He'd swept her onto his lap, smoothed her damp hair from her face, and begun to feed her tidbits, as though she were a fledgling tumbled too soon from the nest. All the time, in the background, her grandfather had snored.

Alexander had torn hunks from the warm inside of the loaf and pressed crumbs of soft white cheese onto them. She had wrinkled up her nose, protesting that she could see a gray thumbprint on the cheese, but she'd eaten his offerings all the same and they had continued with their incomprehensible men's stories and their jokes which she never understood. As they laughed, she relented and laughed too, laughing as loudly as any of them, in the end. The best jokes had been about snoring but she'd forgotten the details. She only remembered that she'd laughed so much she couldn't stop, and had choked on a flake of crust.

Her mother, Vera, had put the knife down on the chopping board and picked her out of Alexander's arms. She'd bathed

Nina's face with cold water from the kitchen tap and her roughened hands had smelled of onion and mint. The water had run down her chin and neck and soaked her pajama top and when she'd torn it off they had all laughed at her even more. All the time, in the other room, her grandfather had snored steadily.

As she grew up she had learned to stand her ground among all those young men, remarking sharply that they should listen to themselves snoring for a change! Then, one summer, she and Anja, her cousin from Sarajevo, who was older than she was, had crept into Alexander's room and left a switched-on tape recorder just under his bed. It had been such a delicious revenge because he hadn't just snored, he'd farted too and they'd had hysterics when they heard that. They had replayed that tape all summer and nearly died of laughter. They had even plotted to send a copy to some girl he was dating at the university. They couldn't imagine that anything could ever be funnier.

And in all those years, summer and winter, in their apartment in town and in this old house in the country, her grandfather's stately snore had always droned through the rooms like a bumblebee trapped by a closed autumn window. And she had never been disturbed by it.

It was why he had refused to sleep in the cellars with everyone else during the siege. He would have betrayed their presence immediately, he always explained. But that wasn't the only reason why he objected to the cellars. Nowadays the special forces didn't even bother to search them. They just tossed in a couple of grenades, then slammed the doors shut and ran.

"I won't be trapped," her grandfather said, "not like that."

Since returning to this house at the end of last year, Nina and her grandfather had slept out on the veranda at the back, even though it had been bitterly cold. And even though they might be back in their own home again, he refused to let her settle in. He insisted that they must always be ready to move on: within the blink of an eyelid they must be on their feet, bag in hand. They must run with no backward glance.

She supposed that he was right, but she hated it. If he'd had his way, she'd have slept with her shoes on, as he did. But she also knew of so many people who had turned back or had lingered too long. They had paused for that one moment to straighten a cloth, to put a lid on a saucepan, to snatch up another jacket, to have a last glimpse of a home before they closed the door. People said that that was what Anja and her mother had done: they had run back for Anja's music certificates, because they would be needed when the war was over and she applied for a scholarship to the music college. They had only been in the drawing room for five seconds, grabbing the envelope from the top drawer in the desk, when the bombardment had begun again. And they had died there, caught in the blast.

Now, in the darkness beyond, the men had stopped on the track. That would be because of the landslide. It had carried away the footbridge over the stream and part of the path. The previous autumn, just before they returned, there had been two weeks of firing from the other side of the valley. Several shells had overshot the main road and hit the hillside and a couple of them had exploded. A month ago, after a week of heavy rain accompanying the thaw, the house had suddenly seemed to stir. Every timber had creaked and the doors had swung. Then they'd heard a sound like an immense dry wave sweeping in from the sea. When it stopped, they had climbed to the attic and looked down. Part of the hillside had fallen away.

Where there had always been a wide, grassy way through the forest and where wild lavender and daisies grew, now there was a huge, rust-colored gash which steamed in the watery sunlight. It was hideous and she could not quite believe it had happened.

At first her grandfather would not let her go out of the garden gate in case the surrounding ground was unstable. Now, in the warm sun of early summer, a fine dusting of new grass was already softening the outlines of the scar on the mountainside.

In one way the landslide had made their position more secure: no vehicles could now go up or down the track, and people who were walking had to pass single file, and with care, around the edge. The problem was that her grandfather had planned for them to use that way through the woods as an escape route, should the front line shift back in their direction. They had even hidden stores at a couple of places on the way down. Now these things were lost too and she had burst into tears as they peered out of the attic window at the fresh devastation of huge boulders split and pine trees torn up by their roots.

"Stupid, stupid men," she'd cried and would have gone on, but her grandfather had stopped her.

"Some of this was begun long before any of them thought to

fight," he said slowly. "See? Look there, and *there!*" He had elbowed her aside as he pointed to the other swathes that had been cut through the forests for the ski runs of the winter season.

"We've already weakened the land. We've worked it too hard. We should have known that this would happen. You can no more tear strips from a mountainside than you can peel the bark from a cherry tree. In the end both will die. We were all too greedy. Much too greedy."

She had turned away from him and sat down on one of the trunks stored in the attic. She didn't agree. Her life hadn't felt greedy. It had felt wonderful, and nobody had loved the mountains more than her family. They had been coming up to this mountain house ever since she could remember. In winter they had been able to ski and toboggan from their back door right down to the village below. It had been like having their very own ski run, sweeping through the silent pines which now and then acknowledged their passing by loosing great boughfuls of sparkling snow. It had been so beautiful, and she pitied her grandfather for not appreciating it.

Last winter, well, the last winter before the outbreak of war, when she was eleven, she'd skied down at night, for the first time, with all the grownups, and she'd carried her own lantern. There had been dozens of other skiers: both local people from the farms and villages, whom she'd known for years, and Yugoslav tourists from cities like Zagreb and Belgrade. There had even been foreigners who came from abroad for the winter sports. Nina had spoken a bit of English to an American girl, and been understood, and they'd skied down side by side.

It had been almost the best thing she'd ever done and it hadn't felt greedy at all, whatever her grandfather said. It had been magical, with the stars as bright as fairy-story diamonds in the sky. The snow at the edges of the forest had not been black but blue, like the depths of the sea. It had been like a scene from one of the fairy stories her father had told her. It was the way life was, or should be, and for a moment she had hated her grandfather, who was always so unromantic and so practical. His wants were so few and had nothing of magic in them. She supposed it was because he was so old. She suspected that old men didn't dream. Yet he had never been like other old men, keeping quiet, and sitting in the corner of a café with their white-haired friends, playing chess and reading the newspapers. He should have resigned himself to old age and let younger, more enthusiastic people dream and enjoy themselves. And he should have let her go through some of her mother's things which were stored up here, in the attic. Somehow or other she had actually grown taller in the last year, and she was sure that there were lots of clothes both in the trunks and in her parents' locked room which she could have worn. He said it was too risky to linger in the upper rooms.

On the day of the landslide she had sulked and absolutely refused to leave the attic, saying that he must leave her alone because she had things to do, private things, that he wouldn't understand. He'd protested but finally gone away. Then she'd spied on him from the attic windows as he broke up more of the furniture for firewood. He took the drawers from the chest in the hall and smashed them to pieces with ease. Recently he'd started to cut his hair, mustache, and beard with a pair of her mother's embroidery scissors. The results were uneven and comic but he didn't mind. He was more afraid, he said, of lice, with so little water and so much hair. He had wanted to shorten her hair further, but she wouldn't let him and was bitter that, despite the deprivations, his ridiculous haircut and the strengthening sun had changed his appearance from that of a frail old man in his seventies to someone much tougher and younger. Now he resembled the fighter he'd been fifty years ago when he'd joined Tito's partisans in these same mountains to battle the Nazi invaders. Nobody watching him swing the ax would have thought him that old.

She had stayed in the attic most of that day, mesmerized by the unaccustomed warmth of the shaft of sunlight that fell through the high, unbroken window. She sniffed the dust and dug her thumbnail into a trickle of resin that had oozed from the window frame. Then she had smelled something else that reminded her of apples, but when she searched she couldn't find any. It had been really warm up there and the sound of gunfire, when she heard it at all, had been very faint indeed.

When this war was over, when there were streets again in Sarajevo with smooth pavements outside, and lit-up shop windows, she knew exactly what she was going to do. She'd hurry straight to the pharmacy, not the one on their street because the assistants knew her there and might ask what she wanted it for. No, she'd go to the one across town, near the library, and she'd buy a bottle of hydrogen peroxide. Then she'd bleach her hair. She'd been thinking about it for ages. It was really unfair that Alexander should be the only one in the family to have such beautiful blond hair, whereas she, the only girl, was as dark as a rat. But she was going to change that. It was one of many outrageous changes that she and Anja had always plotted when their families met up on holidays. They had only been waiting, waiting a bit longer, until they were older. Then they were going to scandalize everyone. She could imagine how heads would turn as she strolled by, and it wouldn't just be her hair which people stared at. It would be her, too. Only now she'd have to do it all on her own.

She had sprawled in the pool of sunlight on the attic floor, rereading childhood books and comics which had been packed away for years. In some of the older ones her father's name was carefully written in a boy's awkward, inky hand. He had always drawn three thick lines underneath his signature, and all were slightly crooked. She could imagine him hunched over these books, even then a tall, ungainly, and serious boy who already dreamed of a future life of scholarship and libraries and re-spectful students. Apparently his nickname had been "Pro-fessor" in primary school, even though his writing wasn't straight.

Sometimes, helplessly, guiltily, she was glad that he was not with them now. He was so impractical that he would have been hopeless at all this. He would have made it even more difficult. Whereas her mother, Vera . . .

On the veranda she eased an edge of blanket up over her mouth. All around it was a clear, cold night. When they got up there might be dew on the ground. Now, in the distance, a dog howled and after a few moments another answered. On the other mattress, under a mound of covers, her grandfather stirred and swallowed and sighed in his sleep, and then re-sumed his snoring.

Those men on the track must have negotiated the landslide because she could not hear them any longer. They must have gone on up to the deserted farms. Nina turned over onto her stomach and snuggled down, searching for more warmth among the bedding.

Then, very very slowly, with her eyes wide open in the dark, she rolled herself silently over onto her back again, and began to reach down for her shoes. She had heard something else.

Maybe it wasn't dogs howling. People round about had reported seeing wolves again. They had been disturbed and driven from their secret places in the mountains by the war and were said to be thriving. For, of course, now there were refugees and livestock wandering and losing their way in the treacherous places where only wolves had gone before. Some people reported seeing packs of them, yellow-eyed and swollen-bellied, slinking back at dawn after a night's work.

2

HAIL IN SPRING

SUDDENLY SOMEONE STUMBLED over one of the flow-erpots which they always left out in odd places along the path which led to the back of the house. It was an old trick, her grandfather said, a partisan's trick. A tin can or an empty beer bottle gave better warning of intruders than many look-outs—and they never complained about the rain. Now some-one coming along their path had stumbled and cursed. She heard the earthenware slide across the concrete and crack. Then she heard the sound of fingers feeling a more cautious way around the corner of the house, slithering lightly over the boarding.

"Grandpa!" Fear rushed at her and overwhelmed her.

She wanted it to be over, for there to be no more of this. Ever.

"Grandpa!" She bit into the rough edge of the blanket.

"Hush, Nina. Hush!"

When she dared to look at him, her grandfather was already on his feet. His gun was already in his hand although she had not heard the click of the safety catch. Had he been awake and waiting there for some time? Could she have slept so long and so deeply?

"Who is there?" His voice was as calm as if he thought a neighbor might have come round on a visit.

"Who is it?" he repeated. "Will you come up?" Though, of course, no one could because there were no steps. He had removed them months ago, as soon as they found their way back to the house.

He had decided, straight away, that they must live on the veranda at the back of the house, because it faced away from the main road in the valley. That was where the fighting had been, and would be again, he calculated, if the situation changed. The gun-emplacements were on the other side of the valley, so if a shell fired from there did hit the house it would have to pass through two rooms before it reached them, on the veranda. It was, therefore, relatively safe; but he'd taken the steps down at once so that they could not be surprised or trapped. It was what he feared most. They had a ladder and a knotted rope, but kept both drawn up.

Outside someone else tripped and swore and when her grandfather asked again who was there, a voice that Nina almost knew called back through the chill night air:

"Grandpa? Grandpa? Is that you?"

"Who is there? One moment, just one moment, if you please." The tone of her grandfather's voice had changed, had cooled, and Nina recognized the change. This was the voice he sometimes used for particularly restless patients. Now she saw him strike one of their precious matches and a dim yellow flame swung and spat as it gripped the homemade wick of the little oil lamp.

She watched the guttering flame move to the corner of the veranda farthest away from where she lay. They never held any light directly in their hands, but always on the end of a stick that he had adapted especially for this. It was another of those old tricks of war: if a sniper were taking aim he would expect to fire a little to the left of a light, where he calculated that the body of a right-handed person might be.

She could see her grandfather's outline now and suddenly was aware that it wasn't the oil lamp which illuminated him. Dawn was breaking. How had she slept so long? Had she fallen asleep after first hearing the men go up the track? Were these the same men? It felt as though only a moment had passed. Had her grandfather been awake and keeping guard for most of the night?

"Grandpa Fikret? It's me, Fahro! I'm with friends, Grandpa."

"Fahro? You astonish me!"

Fahro! So he was safe! Yet it did not seem to Nina that her grandfather was experiencing the rush of delight that she felt. Her cousin Fahro! No one had heard of him for months and the worst was feared. Her grandfather had even spoken of him with indifference, assuming that he had already been killed. He did not seem to remember that before the outbreak of war Fahro had been one of her brother's best friends and that he had shared all their lives. Poor Fahro. Her joy was mixed with

16

fear. Whatever should she say to him, now, about his mother and his sister Anja? Did he even know?

"Can we come up? Grandpa Fikret?" Fahro shouted.

Fikret Topič did not reply at once. Instead he hurried over to where his granddaughter lay, pushed her shoes and bag out of sight, and roughly dragged the blanket from between her teeth and flung it right over her face to cover her completely. Then he put something on top, just as though she wasn't even there.

"We need to come up, Dr. Topič. Now." This was another, older voice.

Then she heard the rattle of the ladder. Poor old Fahro: it really wasn't fair. Her grandfather had never approved of him because he played in a rock band in Sarajevo and was, in the old man's opinion, a "bum" and a "hippie." Nina, however, had always liked him a lot and could have fancied him if he hadn't been her first cousin and Anja's brother. Once, at a wedding, he'd bought her a drink and asked her to dance and she'd nearly died of excitement at the touch of his hand and the beat of the music and the knowledge that people were watching them. He was so good-looking, though she wasn't sure why, and such fun. And now he had no one.

The blanket had scratched her cheek and left grit and pieces of fluff in her mouth. She needed to spit them out, but didn't dare. She feared that they might choke her and that no one would know, that she would suffocate, there and then, with this great, thick weight pressing down all over her.

Then the men were climbing up onto the veranda. Fahro was introducing their grandfather, Dr. Fikret Topič, to the men he was with; he was describing them as "great friends and great fighters." An unexpected silence seemed to follow this introduction. Her grandfather did not seem to be speaking, to be returning their greetings. He did not ask Fahro how he was; he did not even ask if he had news of her brothers.

Eventually Nina heard them begin to move around again; a chair was dragged over and someone sat down on it heavily. Another settled on the end of her mattress and seemed quite unaware that he was pinning her ankles one on top of the other. It was an undignified and ludicrous position to be in and she resented it. It also began to hurt.

Then Fahro broke into the renewed silence. He was speaking too loudly and too fast and seemed unable to stop.

"Of course, I haven't been back to this house for years! Years and years. I can't remember the last time—I must have been just a kid, right, Grandpa? That's why I didn't recognize it at once. Especially with the landslide. That's just awful. And what a mess. Whenever did it happen? Lucky the old house didn't slide down too, very lucky, eh, Grandpa?"

No one interrupted him.

"Of course, I didn't think you'd be here. Grandpa—never dreamed you'd be around—"

"Why not? It's my home."

"Yes. Oh, yes. I mean, Dad always said that the house had been in the family for ages, even though we don't know who owned the land before. I didn't mean *that*. I meant . . . it being still winter. I didn't expect you to be here in winter. Though winter's nearly ended. Hasn't it? Now, of course, summer's different. You should see this house in summer: now, that's really something, with the cherry trees. All the houses round here have cherry trees. It's the soil, isn't it, Grandpa? It grows the best cherries ever. How many trees have you got? Five? Six? And all different types. It's amazing, absolutely amazing, you can have cherries all year round here. Well, all summer, that is. Though there's cherry jam and cherry tart and cherry brandy. Now, that *is* something. That'll get you going. And I bet there's still a few bottles, still hidden away, eh, Grandpa?"

"They are not hidden, Fahro. They are in the cabinet in the dining room, where they always were."

"Really? Now, that *is* amazing. Some things never change! So, what I said was true: it's cherries all the year round up here, even if some of them are in brandy. And of course, there's the blossom in spring. In spring—" Then he stopped his desperate chatter.

Had he remembered too? Had he recalled that day in spring, the last spring before the war? Anja had been the age that Nina was now, though she had been much taller then than Nina was ever likely to be. That day it had hailed briefly in the middle of a sunny afternoon. The whole family had been in the house, gathered there for some holiday or maybe a spring break, she couldn't remember exactly. And maybe Alexander hadn't been there, because he was already doing his military service, but the rest of them were there, including Fahro, together with friends from the farms around. Anyway, sudden hail had covered the spring pastures, rattled on the roof, bounced off the boards of the veranda, and dashed the blossom from the cherry trees.

Afterward, she and Anja had run out to investigate this freak of nature. They'd swept up handfuls, armfuls of the soft, pink blossom with bits of ice hidden within, like a million cold, white pearls. They'd thrown them at each other, jumping from terrace to terrace beneath the trees, covering themselves in the chilled, faintly scented flowers. Then Fahro and Nina's brother Samir, and Slobo from the next farm, had all come out of the house and joined in. The youths had ganged up on Anja. They'd rolled her in the flowers, piling them over her, and tossing them in her hair until finally she begged for mercy. Then they'd stopped and pulled her to her feet with hands that were cold and smeared with mud and grass. Nina had watched Anja brushing the cherry blossom from her long dark hair, and just for one moment she had so longed to be her.

Oh, Anja.

Her ankles hurt now, really hurt. And this man, whoever he was, was definitely a pig. He probably knew that he was hurting her and was enjoying it. Because some of those fighting the war definitely enjoyed hurting people, everybody agreed about that. "The kids"—that's what people in Sarajevo had been calling these men who talked of peace by day and sharpened their knives at night. They were like the bullies at school who always smiled shyly at somebody else's tears and acted as though they were surprised.

Oh, Anja.

Sometimes, in a hateful, burning fever of guilt, she missed her cousin Anja more than she missed her parents: she would have moved forward with Anja and her parents would have been left behind. When Anja got her place in music school in Sarajevo, as she would, because all sorts of people considered her to be seriously talented, a natural cellist, they said—when Anja got her place, Nina was going to join her. They would share an apartment in the student quarter of the city and Nina would study literature at the university. It was all planned. They'd have a kitten and red geraniums on the old iron balcony. They'd sit out there in the sun, among the lines of flapping washing and the wine bottles, and they'd have lots of friends, real student friends. Then Nina would begin her novel, the proper novel that she knew she would write, when she was older. It would make her famous and it wouldn't be trashy and imaginary like the stuff she wrote now. And it wouldn't be anything at all like the fairy stories and folk tales which her father collected. She would never write anything that began "Once upon a time in a faraway land." No, hers would be real: a novel about real life. Or a play. But whichever it was, she'd always imagined herself reading passages out to Anja. Anja would have listened and understood and wouldn't have criticized, or not like teachers do, always fussing over spelling mistakes.

People would have pointed them out in the cafés in Sarajevo. They'd say, "Do you know who those two girls are? No? Well, the little one is Nina Topič, the girl who wrote that novel, and the tall one is her cousin Anja Bokar, the cellist." And complete strangers would ask to be introduced to them. Having Anja as a cousin had been even better than having a sister because Nina had noticed that sisters often quarreled dreadfully, whereas she and Anja had never quarreled once, in all their lives.

Oh, Anja. She missed her so much. And so must Fahro, if he knew.

Anja's elder brother Fahro had always dreamed of going to America. He'd talked about it since he was a little boy. He'd been desperate to leave Yugoslavia and wanted to go to California and that was another reason why her grandfather disapproved of him. But Nina didn't. She sympathized with his dreams. Now she knew that he'd been right. He should have gone and he should have taken Anja with him.

Now some of the other men were talking again. They spoke of the war, naturally, and were asking her grandfather what he, Dr. Fikret Topič, thought about it.

"Me?" the old man asked sharply. "Me? Since when have any of you cared for the opinions of people like me?"

She sensed their surprise. This was her grandfather's private voice; this was the way he spoke in the safety of family and friends. In public he had always been so careful, so controlled. She did not understand what had changed him. She felt a sudden deepening of fear, as if a blow had struck an unhealed wound.

"Come now, Dr. Topič—" The man who had been on the end of her mattress got up as he spoke. She resisted the intense desire to gasp out loud, to reach down and rub away some of the pain in her legs.

Then another laughed loudly and scornfully.

"Who is this stupid old man, anyway?"

"I've told you who he is. He's my grandfather, my mother's father, Dr. Fikret Topič—" Fahro's voice was shrill and tight with terror.

"Shut your mouth, Fahro! Shut your stupid lying mouth, can't you?"

"Sorry. I'm sorry, Branko."

"See? Didn't I warn you about these scum from Sarajevo? They're not real people at all! They're animals! Sheep—shout

22

at them and they cringe. And you, old man, call yourself a doctor, do you? Then what do you think you're doing here sitting in comfort in your country house, while good men, our fighters and brothers, are dying because there are not enough doctors to treat their wounds. Call yourself a doctor? Then where's your white coat, old man? Come on, let's see it. Let's see if you've got a doctor's white coat hidden under all these jackets!"

The voice was mocking and panting with anger. She heard the clatter of boots and a chair overturned and her grandfather protest. She heard him shout out. Then someone fell and groaned and while Fahro screamed someone else was grunting with satisfaction each time he kicked.

When Nina flung the blanket aside and ran between them, her grandfather was on his knees in a corner of the veranda. A couple of men were tearing off his jacket and sweater.

"Don't you hurt my grandfather, you pig, you filthy son of a pig!" She seized hold of one of the men's arms but he stood up and casually flung her aside and returned to the attack.

Fahro was shaking like a child, holding out his arms and crying, "No, no," between chattering teeth. Then a tall man who had been sitting there, watching it all, ordered them to stop. He came over to Nina and smiled and held out his hand to pull her to her feet. When she wouldn't move he grabbed her wrist, and jerked her up.

"Well, well, Dr. Topič. What good fortune to have a little friend like this, in such troubled times. But *is* she friendly, Dr. Topič? Or is she as unfriendly as she looks: is she a bad girl, after all?"

The four strangers who were with Fahro now turned to look

at Nina. The tall man did not let go of her wrist but righted a chair and forced her down into it. A red sun swung over the top of the mountains opposite and in its clear dawn light she saw her grandfather wipe the blood from his mouth. The strangers looked quickly at one another and then back at her.

3

WHERE THE WOLVES GO

THE THREE YOUNGER MEN were long-haired with straggling mustaches and dark, uneven beards clinging to their chins and throats. One, a shorter, stouter man, was hung around with ammunition belts, and even then, even in that dreadful moment when she was aware that she had somehow made their situation more dangerous and more desperate, even then, as she glanced at this man with his chestful of gleaming bullets, she thought how stupid he looked: he was really and truly stupid, like some overgrown kid, dressed up. As his fingers scratched tenderly around in the lank hair on the back of his head, she was reminded of a nest full of plump baby rats. She could hear him, hear his nails picking away at something on his scalp, and she was revolted.

The tall man released her wrist and stepped back. His brown hair was cropped very short but his mustache was thick and full and sprouted from skin that was deeply sunburned and lined all over with a mesh of deep wrinkles. She was familiar with that sort of face with its deep-set eyes and prominent, bony nose. It was the face of the farmers and shepherds who had always worked the land around here: tall, gaunt men, with immense, fleshy palms to their hands. Their necks, bent for many years under the sun, were a rough, grainy red, like slabs of meat cut open on the butcher's block. It had always been difficult to guess at their age and this man, as she sought to avoid his eyes, could have been as young as thirty or as old as sixty. There was something shut in and too quiet about these men, something you could never know. At the neck of his shirt she glimpsed a gold chain and crucifix, and a knife was stuck in his belt.

In the corner her grandfather was staggering to his feet, pulling himself up on the side of the veranda. His shirt gaped where they'd tried to rip it off. His hands shook as he held the edges together.

"Let me," he said, in a voice which he barely managed to steady, "let me introduce my granddaughter, Nina Topič, to you. Nina? Say hello . . . to the gentlemen . . ."

Instantly she understood, from his tone, what part she must play and now she grinned childishly up at them, pushing her hair out of her eyes and swinging her legs, which were clad in rolled-up striped pajamas tucked into thick socks. Fahro stared at her as though turned to stone; his hands were outstretched and his mouth was open and moving but his eyes were quite dark and still, as though he were not seeing her at all. She did not like to see him like that.

"Fahro? Fahro, can you come here?" Dr. Topič was struggling to speak now. When her cousin still didn't respond, Nina caught her grandfather's eye and offered herself instead.

"Let me, Grandfather . . . Shall I . . . do something?"

"Yes. Thank you, Nina. Just fetch a tray, dear, and glasses for our guests." He coughed painfully. "And cheese. Do we still have that cheese?"

"I'm not sure. I'll look, shall I?"

She got up and walked through the group of men and into the house. Her heart beat so wildly that it consumed and deafened her. As she crouched by the cabinet and slid open the dusty glass doors she was aware that the men on the veranda were talking again, but she couldn't understand what they were saying. This other, overwhelming banging in her head obliterated all other sounds.

She unscrewed the cap of the bottle and smelled the sharp, familiar scent of other times; then, squatting down in the shadows of the abandoned room, she spat quickly into four of the glasses and carefully poured the cherry brandy on top.

Surely her grandfather didn't seriously intend her to offer these vile men any of their precious cheese? But he did, and sent her away irritably "to look again" when she'd handed round the glasses. As she went back into the house one of the men put out his hand and touched her arm and laughed when she scowled at him. From within the dark room, where everything that had been so nice was now spoiled and stank of ruin and neglect, she heard them begin to talk more loudly and easily. One of them must have made a joke because they all laughed and among their laughter she thought she heard her grandfather, joining in, faintly, at the end.

She put their last piece of cheese on a plate, then couldn't bear it and cut it in two, hiding the smaller piece in her pajama pocket. What was left didn't look very generous and she was glad but her grandfather was inexplicably angry with her.

"You little *fool*," he said unpleasantly when she held out the plate. "Don't you ever do as you're told? Go away and get the *good* cheese! Go and look properly this time. And don't come back until you've found it! Do you understand?"

"But, Grandfather—" she tried to protest because there never had been any other cheese and he knew that, but he raised his hand. He made as if to strike her, to hit her across the face, which he had never done before, never even seemed likely to do, until now. She flinched away in horror and ran back inside the house.

How could he? Especially when he knew, he absolutely knew, that there wasn't any other cheese. Had they hurt his brain when they kicked him? Or was he, finally, losing his wits, like everyone else? Was he leaving her too, even after promising that he never, ever would? Was he about to join those who had already disappeared into death or insanity in this never-ending war? Her parents, her brothers, Anja—they'd all gone now. They'd all left her and this house, where once they'd been so happy. If this was what her grandfather was doing, then she hated him for it; hated him even more because she had trusted him. He had always promised and she, despite all, had always trusted him when he had said that he would save her.

Now, desperate to get away from him and from the

strangers, she made her way up the stairs; she paused to listen for their voices, then went on, past the closed rooms, up through the center of the emptied house and on to the attic right at the top. Here hardly any sound at all could reach her. How could he do that? She walked over to the little, slanting window in the roof and rubbed a circle free of dust with the elbow of her sweater. There wasn't any point in looking for the cheese, but she'd pretend to, in case he was angry again, and anyway, it was much warmer here than on the veranda.

Why had he done that to her? Made her look such a fool, when she wasn't. And nearly hit her . . . She stared out over the valley and was startled anew by the landslide. Each time it was as though she'd almost forgotten it again, as though in the middle of the night something magic might have happened and straightened out the chaos of the ugly, torn-out stones, broken-limbed trees, and the suffocating red mud. Often she dreamed that the grassy slope had been restored and once she dreamed that she and Anja were sprawled there together, bare-legged among the scented spears of lavender and the little, sunny faces of marigolds. They had lain there side by side with the hot sun on their skin and there had been scarcely any sound at all, except the summer drone of wild honeybees, which Anja had once said sounded like the cello . . .

Now down in the valley nothing moved. The main road was deserted. A couple of weeks ago an aid convoy had made its slow way along, being stopped every kilometer or so by roadblocks. Their cheese had come from its load. Without it they would have starved. Then Nina and her grandfather had expected the big guns hidden in the forests opposite to open up, but they hadn't, or at least not until the trucks had passed and then it had only been a couple of shells neatly positioned to remind everyone who was really in control. She was sure that the snipers hidden in the caves would never have lifted their sights from the vehicles and could have blown them to pieces at any moment—and might have them trained on her, at this very moment!

She ducked beneath the windowsill, appalled by her own carelessness. How could she have done that? Was she imitating her grandfather and becoming stupid and careless too? That had been one of the earliest lessons of this war: never to stand for long at a window. If you are to survive, her grandfather always said, you can decide to take some risks, but you must never take a chance. Standing by a window and looking at a view was definitely taking an unnecessary chance. But why had he taken just such a chance with these men? Why had he spoken of his true feelings of despair at this war? They had had other fighters in the house and he'd never talked like that. Was it exhaustion? Boredom? Or just the frailty of old age? Because he was old, whatever he and she pretended.

She crawled across the floor on hands and knees and listened at the top of the stairs. There was nothing but their distant voices. No one was coming up after her. Now that they had their cherry brandy and their men's talk of war, they seemed to have forgotten all about her. Typical.

She crawled back into the attic and very carefully closed and locked the door. When she was little, this was where she and Anja had come when they wanted to play girls' games. They had hidden themselves up here away from the boys and the men and they'd talked about private things. They'd unpacked some of the boxes and trunks and tried on the ludicrously old-fashioned clothes and hats that had been stored away. She had been overcome with excitement and envy at the sight of Anja's more grown-up body and disappointed at the way nothing ever fitted her. She was too small and thin.

At one time some of the uniform her grandmother had worn when she'd fought with the partisans had been carefully folded away up here in mothballs and tissue paper. They'd never dared try that on, though they had untied the string, lifted the lid, and touched the fabric beneath. Then, guiltily, they had tried to retie the bow in exactly the same way. It had been a pale green box, she was sure of that: a flat, pale green box with a white label at one corner with her grandfather's bold writing on it. It was probably still here. The family always said that Nina was very like this grandmother who had died so young at the end of the last war. Her grandfather still carried a photo of her in his wallet, though it was now so cracked and aged you could barely make her out at all.

A pile of skis stood in one corner and there, beside them, was her doll's stroller with its red-checked pillow and blanket. She'd wanted a stroller so much, then she barely played with it because her brothers had teased her so dreadfully, whizzing it between them like a racing car so that the babies shot out onto the floor. And there, too, was the little toy stove which her grandfather had made for her birthday. Her fourth? Fifth? She'd played with that a lot. She clearly remembered cooking up flowers and leaves and transforming them, with just a dash of rainwater and a sprinkling of soil, into cakes and almond cookies and crunchy cheese pies which everybody had said were absolutely delicious. She reached out and clicked the little blue knobs which had turned on the burners. The saucepans must be somewhere as well. Her mother had bought them for her and it had been such a surprise. They hadn't been cheap plastic ones from the bazaar, they'd been miniatures of the real things, made of metal and with proper lids and handles, and had been made abroad. She had liked them so much.

Then she saw the corner of the box. She had to jerk it free from the pile of magazines on top and when the string broke, she dropped it and the contents tumbled out over the floor. She listened at the door once more but no one seemed to have heard. There was the jacket: she peeled off her own sweater and thrust her hands into the cold, flattened sleeves and eased it over her shoulders. So it was true. She was, it seemed, very like her grandmother in build. The jacket was a bit big, because now she was so thin, but it wasn't so bad. It was a shame there was no mirror in the attic. She began to do up the awkward, old-fashioned buttons and as she did so she felt a rustle of paper in one of the pockets.

She took out an envelope containing two letters, both with smudged foreign stamps, and then three small black-and-white photographs, folded inside some sort of ticket. She turned them over curiously. Those, surely, were English stamps, with that English Queen's head.

"Dear Vera," she read, with her finger on each word. Here it was again at the beginning of the other letter: "My dearest Vera." How strange that her mother had never mentioned this good friend in England. Two of the photos were of Alexander.

He was scowling into the sun, with one arm across his brow, casting a shadow over his face, but his wide, friendly smile was clearly visible. He seemed to be on a beach. He was wearing flared jeans and a patterned shirt which she didn't remember; it must have been taken when he was in Dubrovnik several summers ago. She'd heard that he'd got up to all sorts of things down there, but had his hair really been that long?

"My dearest Vera . . . I . . . have . . . I have . . . not." Maybe she shouldn't read it. Had it been hidden up here, or just forgotten?

She had never thought of her mother as a woman with secrets. Her father, Georg Topič, possibly. He, after all, had been a professional dreamer, a writer and collector of fabulous stories who had always seemed more at ease with the witches and kings and talking foxes of the fairy tales than with the struggles of everyday family life. Sometimes, when he returned in the evenings, after a day teaching Shakespeare to reluctant students, her father would find them all at home sitting around the kitchen table, talking all at once. Then he used to look at them with amazement as though he had forgotten he had this family at all.

Maybe this friendship of her mother's was one that had gone wrong. Maybe they had stopped being friends and that was why it had never been mentioned.

"My dearest Vera, I have not for–got–ten you and . . ."

She heard something from downstairs. With any luck Fahro's rough friends were finally going. They had had a drink and a bit of fun and now they were off. When they had gone, then she could slip down and ask Fahro to translate the letter for her. It wouldn't be a problem for him, because his English was wonderful, everybody said so. He'd learned it all from pop songs and tourists.

Somewhere below, somebody laughed so loudly and suddenly that the end of the noise trailed up to her like a distant howl. It must have been some quite disgusting joke. She felt offended that her grandfather seemed to have forgotten about her so completely. Normally he would never have let her stay up here on her own.

Yet something was not quite right. She looked back at the things in her hand. There was still something odd about those photographs of Alexander. She held them toward the shaft of light from the little window and noticed the girl who was standing just behind Alexander. Her determined gaze into the glare of the sun reminded Nina of something. It was almost within her grasp. This girl was not shading her eyes. If the photograph had only been clearer, she could have seen.

Then she heard the shots. She felt one round of automatic gunfire swing and tear through the house. And then another. From very close by, and most unusually for such a bright summer morning, a wolf began to howl. It was still howling as she hurriedly pulled her sweater back on over the jacket.

Minutes later, as she squeezed herself down into the thick, black webs of dirt between one of the trunks and the wall, she thought she heard the wolf dragging itself slowly up the stairs. It was coming toward her but it wasn't howling now. It was panting and gasping for breath. She heard its claws scratching across the boards and then, as she tried to make herself invisible, to vanish absolutely and forever, she heard its teeth close around the handle of the door. She imagined how its red tongue would curl and quiver in delight and how some of its saliva would splash down into the dust. Its yellow eyes would flicker as it caught her scent, and however still she kept, it would know she was there.

4

IN THE HEAT OF THE DAY

S HE DID NOT KNOW how long she had been holding her breath.

"Anja? Are you there, Anja? An–ja!"

Nina still didn't move, just crouched there behind the trunk with eyes very firmly shut and her breath held in so tightly that for a few moments she seemed to float away. She was no longer sure of what had happened.

"Anja?"

Had there been a further burst of shooting? There was another noise, certainly, but maybe it was only the sound of whatever was outside the door and waiting to get in.

"An–ja!" The call was fainter.

She almost replied, almost answered "Yes! Here we are!" and for a second, for one wonderful, secret moment, she thought that she wasn't alone and that Anja's black hair had touched her cheek. Then she remembered.

"Anja?" the voice whimpered. "Please! Please come out. It's only me. It's only your brother, Fahro."

Later, when she dared to move, she knelt by the keyhole and peered out. Fahro was slumped on the top stair, quite alone, with his gun propped up beside him. There were bright drops of blood on the boards. He was rolling up one trouser leg to inspect a wound on his shin. He looked up in bewilderment when she finally unlocked the door.

"Isn't Anja coming?" he asked irritably.

Nina shook her head.

"Well, can't *you* do something?" He was holding the edges of the wound together and when she bent down to see how bad it was, she realized that she still had the envelope clenched in her hand.

He was filthy. She could see the dirt and lice in his matted hair and she could smell him, smell something that caught in her throat and made her turn her head away.

"Fahro—"

He barely acknowledged her but continued to stare with a curious, delighted intensity at his wound, which was not that bad, not compared with some of the things she'd seen. It could not have accounted for the shower of blood that she now saw spattered over his face and neck and chest.

"Fahro? Shall I get you . . . something?"

"All right." He nodded pleasantly but didn't look at her, only bent right over as though he would have touched his mouth to the wound. Then, when she had stepped past him, he began to bang his forehead on the edge of the stair again and again and again.

Step by step she made her way down through the house. She

knew that she mustn't look at anything, not if she could avoid it. They had talked about it so often, or her grandfather had talked and she had listened to him, always agreeing that it was best not to look. She'd even promised, and promised also that if anything like this were to happen, then she would leave the house at once. After all, that was why they each had kept a small bag packed, wasn't it? "Take your bag, if you can, and just go," he had always said. "Don't wait. Not for me, not for anyone. We can always follow. It is the best thing you can do for those who have loved you, Nina. We only want you to go where you will be safe."

She saw him now, sprawled on the floor with his back to the veranda door. There was glass everywhere and piles of plaster where the walls had been hit. But he did not seem to have been cut! Yet his face was different. His skin was pale and drawn. She had never seen him looking like that. It was as though years and years had intervened and he was suddenly, finally, too old. Her bag and shoes were beside him and he glanced at them before looking up at her.

"Nina. You must go now, Nina. You must go into the forest. Now." It was an effort for him to speak. "Spend the day there. Two days, if you need to. Watch what is going on, and whatever you do, you must never come back to this house. Sleep if you can and when you have slept you will be brave enough for anything!" He made it sound possible, easy almost, when really they both knew it wasn't like that at all, that the best and most sensible plans could come to nothing or even worse, in this war. If bravery was all that was required for survival, then all those whom she had known and loved would still be alive, every single one of them.

He shouldn't have talked like that. He, at least, should know better. He should have been speaking to her of luck and guardian angels and magic charms, because that was what people really needed. But that had never been his way. He had always despised anything that was superstitious and magical. And anyway, did he really expect her to go away now, to leave him as though she didn't care, even if she'd always promised that she would? That was so typical of him. He always had to be the one to make the sacrifice, to bear the heaviest burden. Even now, when he was suddenly so old and frail, and in need of help himself, he was still telling her what to do.

"Nina?" His voice was unclear, and suddenly it tailed away.

She screamed, then bit her lips, clamping her hand over her mouth, although it was all too late. She heard herself scream repeatedly, sending this ugly, unwanted sound through every quiet corner of the house. It was as if in a moment of madness she had let a flame touch blowing curtains and now stood aside helplessly, watching the inferno.

"Nina! Hush. I'm all right."

She couldn't stop, couldn't even see him through her tears, and only knew that at last she was sitting beside him on the bottom stair. Somehow, he had forced himself to kneel before her, trying to tie the laces on her shoes just as he had done when she was a little girl and he was getting her ready for school. Then he used to tie them with double knots so that they would stay firmly done up all day. Now his hands trembled so much that he could not do anything at all.

"Nina," he said again, "now is the time for you to go."

"No!" She flung her arms around him, pushing her face into the soft, dry skin of his cheek and throat. "I won't," she breathed, getting closer to him still. "I can't. Don't make me go away. Please."

"Nina. I can't make you go. I only ask."

"No!" She shook her head vigorously and put one hand up and stroked his cheek and tried to make him look at her, tried to make him relent. His skin when she touched him was clammy and cold, as though he had a chill. A nerve under his eye flickered and there was a thin smear of dried blood around his mouth that she would have wiped off, if she could.

He lifted her hand from his face and then reached for the other and held them both enclosed in his as though he had caught a pair of soft winged moths. Then he saw what she was still holding.

He recognized it at once. She watched his face change as an idea formed in his mind.

"That's it," he whispered, "that's where you must go!" He turned the envelope over and pointed to the address. "England. See? That is the town; that, I think, is the name of the house and this is the man—the man who wrote the letter. See? His name is Paul, Paul Fellows. You must go to him and he will help you, Nina."

"But who is he?"

"He was a friend of your parents, from long ago, when they were all young."

"But they never mentioned a friend in England. They never talked about him to me."

"Maybe they forgot."

"Maybe. But—"

"Nina, there is no time left. Not now. You must go at once,

while you can. And this is what you will do. Go up the track, past the landslide and the remains of the bridge, and enter the forest, but on the far side of the stream. Then you will not have problems crossing it later. You follow? Good. Now, another aid convoy will be coming down the road, maybe today, maybe tomorrow, but it will be stopped at the roadblock by the bridge. This is what I have learned from those . . . those men whom Fahro brought to us. That is why they were here, to be able to cover the convoy from both sides of the valley; they will delay it. Some of the aid will be taken from it and then they will turn it back. And when it goes back, Nina, you will go with it."

"How? How can I do that?"

"By asking. That is what you will do. And you will ask nicely, won't you? You will watch and choose someone to ask, someone whom you think will say yes to you. And when you are there, Nina, in England, then you will write a letter to . . . to us, and tell us that you are safe. You understand?"

"Yes. But why don't *you* come too?"

"I?" He smiled then, smiled for the first time in weeks, if not months. "I am too . . . old, Nina. And besides"—he nodded toward the top of the stairs—"whatever would happen to poor Fahro? Eh? It seems that, in the end, he and I must put up with each other, after all." And he smiled again, but without any joy.

He was putting the envelope into her bag, closing the zipper and holding up his face to be kissed as though she would be back in a little while, but he did not get up. When she stepped toward the door into the veranda he held out his arm, barring the way.

"No. Not that way. When you leave my house you must go

by the front door, like a guest, and not like a thief in the night. So, Nina, now is the time for you to go."

So she left him and went to the front door and pulled back the heavy bolts, which they had not done since their return. She stepped out into the amazing brightness of an early summer's day where streaks of white clouds decorated the clear blue sky.

"Go," he whispered, and without looking back she breathed in the fresh, sweet air.

She glanced up and down the track. There were footprints in the mud; there was the broken pot at the side of the path. Outside nothing moved at all. Behind her, in the house, all remained utterly silent. The old lilac by the gate which they had cut and burned in the winter had sent out a few new shoots and between some of them, a yellow-bellied spider had worked its web. Now it hung there in the rising warmth and waited.

By midday she was already making her way through the dappled coolness of the forest. She went as silently as she could, stopping every few minutes to listen and to see if there was anyone else about or anything other than shadows moving from tree to tree. Sometimes, in sudden clearings, there would be patches of lush green grass spotted with early marigolds and daisies. When she paused she would feel the full strength of the sun on her head. Usually, and wherever she could, she stayed in the shadows. Once, through the trees and following the banks of the stream, she saw a trail of plastic bags and bits of clothing caught on the dead black branches of the firs. Farther on there was a blanket and an upturned plastic bowl and a child's little red shoe. The grass was trampled down where people had fallen or maybe run headlong, discarding this, and then that, in their panic to get away—

Which was what she knew she mustn't do. She mustn't panic, nor look back at the fear which padded at her heels and snapped the dried twigs underfoot in a way which made her gasp for breath and wipe the sweat from the back of her neck. She mustn't run, not now, when there was no need.

Up at the house . . . No, that was something else she mustn't do. Once, when she paused to rest, she imagined herself pushing open the veranda door . . . only to discover that the strangers weren't there. The men's bodies weren't sprawled over the mattresses, among the splintered wood and bits of broken bricks, as she had seen them in Sarajevo. They just weren't there at all. Somehow that frightened her even more, and when a squirrel leaped suddenly from one branch to another, overhead, she stopped dead in her tracks and knew, absolutely knew, that at least one of them was close by, even though she couldn't see him. She could feel his hand on her wrist.

But she stopped herself. She wouldn't and mustn't think about what had happened. Not yet. Up at the house . . . there was only the spider turning slowly in its web. She would put the house in some past time that was now very far away. In that past, when she and Anja had been little girls, they would have run out of the front door side by side and taken sticks and poked at the spider until it moved, scrambling quickly and diagonally across the threads and disappearing. Then they would have shrieked and jumped about, shaking out their hair and their shirts, imagining it caught, and not sure where it had got to. When they were little, they had never thought of cruelty and sadness and suffering. She had not even known about things like that: she had been concerned with friends' birthday parties and whether she would be invited or not, and with films and trips out to eat pizza or ice cream, if it was summer. In winter she had wondered when, if ever, she would get new boots and skis of her own. She had grumbled about having to use ones which somebody bigger had grown out of. That had been all she knew of unhappiness. And that was what she would remember: she wouldn't think about what had happened up at the house. Not yet.

Gradually, the shadows were lifting as the forest was thinning out. Now she could see fields beyond and the burned-out shells of farm buildings. That would be Slobo's father's farm. Most of their land was on the higher slopes of the mountain and they had only bought this quite recently. It was better land, watered by the stream and with easy access to the road. Here his family had raised vegetables and melons and salad crops. She used to come down here with her mother to pick peas and beans before the war. Once, she had been stung on the heel by a bee and it had been such agony to walk that Slobo himself had stopped work and carried her home, piggyback. She had clung to his neck so tightly that he'd clowned around, making choking noises and protesting that she wanted to strangle him. Later that evening, even though her foot throbbed dreadfully and she'd had to sit on the sofa with it propped up on a cushion, her mother had still made her help to top and tail the beans so that they could be bottled, ready for winter. That was her mother all over: a sturdy, no-nonsense sort of woman.

Now the fields were deserted. Nothing had been planted for a couple of years. No one looked up from the row he was weeding, or waved and came over to chat and rub the pain in his aching back. Slobo and his father were said to be up in the mountains opposite and the rest of the family had gone away to the safety of Pale or Zagreb or somewhere like that.

She shaded her eyes and looked carefully over the ruins. There was nothing: only a cat on top of one of the walls left standing. It was curled up and fast asleep in the sun. This was where she would stay, not on the farmland itself, because it was too exposed, but here at the edge of the forest. She could watch the road from here. Later, when she was quite sure that no one else was about, she would follow the stream down to where it joined the river, just before the bridge. With any luck she would be protected by its high rocky banks and if she waited until the evening, when the shadows were longer, she might be able to get close to the road without being noticed at all.

But what then? Whatever had her grandfather imagined that she would be able to do then? She crouched down and looked around.

There were butterflies in the field in front, a handful of them, like petals tossed up into the air. There must be grasshoppers too, because she could hear them all around; and that must be the sound of the stream. Its mountain waters would still be ice-cold as they splashed over the stones.

Slobo's family had been building an extension to their house. They were going to take in tourists. Everybody around had been doing it. Skiers came in winter and hikers in the summer. The building work had been going on for years; each summer they added another room and Nina's brothers had often gone down to help mix concrete and plaster the walls. They had come back joking that Slobo was a good farmer but a hopeless builder: tortoises did a faster job of housing themselves. And now it was all gone. All that work was spoiled and suddenly she was glad that she was leaving. She'd never come back, ever, and she couldn't think why she hadn't left before. She'd had opportunities to join an evacuation of children from Sarajevo, but she hadn't wanted to, not even after her parents were killed. Now she didn't understand why she'd refused.

She chose a sheltered place in a ditch behind a dense patch of bramble which would hide her from any snipers up on the hills. Later, when it was cooler, she would make her way over to the stream. For now, while it was so hot, she would lie down, put her head on her bag and stretch out her legs. And anyway, there were no wolves down here, so she could sleep undisturbed. In the heat of the day they would be in the heart of the forest and in the stony places among the mountaintops, or sprawled in the spoiled homes, with their yellow eyes half-closed.

5

ON THE BRIDGE

FOR SEVERAL MINUTES MORE Nina clung on to sleep; she held the distant noise of running engines within a chaotic dream of being back home in the flat in Sarajevo. She was dreaming, absurdly, that their washing machine had been switched on. It was pounding round and round on the spin cycle and the noise was so loud that the whole building shook with the vibrations. She was seated at the kitchen table trying to finish homework and was disturbed by the racket but was unable to do anything about it. When she looked at the machine she saw that there were rocks inside, instead of clothes. Broken bricks and roof tiles rather than shirts and socks crashed against the round glass window in the door in a wild sea of soapy suds. She was aware that rocks might need to be washed clean but she couldn't bear the noise and she was fearful that at any moment the glass would shatter. She begged her father to do something but he didn't or couldn't. Nothing would happen, he said: didn't she realize that he was fully occupied cleaning his pen? Now she noticed that he was bent over the kitchen sink, washing the clogged nib of his fountain pen in a dribble of water from the tap. Didn't she know, he asked, that writers' pens get easily blocked with too many words? These words dry up and stop the flow and have to be scratched off.

She looked back at the washing machine. It was a little quieter. Then she saw that the rocks were gone. They had been replaced by gold pen nibs: shoals of them clattered and scraped against the glass like stiff little fish. She was mildly surprised by this but was more irritated by the fact that her father had been right after all. The glass had held. The noise had definitely changed and so had the water. It was running inexplicably close by. She dreamed that she could almost reach out to it. She could have dipped a cupped hand into it and let the water that was now clear and ice-cold slip between her lips and run down her throat, but something impossibly and immovably heavy prevented her from moving.

When Nina finally woke, her mouth was swollen and sour with thirst. One of her arms was numb where she had lain upon it. Now she realized that the noise which had finally broken through her dream came from a line of trucks waiting on the road beyond the farm. Their engines were still running. She jumped up in sudden horror, wondering if she dared make an open run for it. Suppose they drove off? They could have already been standing there for hours. They might just rev up and move off without her.

Then she'd be lost. She'd have to make her way back up to the house and she couldn't do that, not now. And not ever. She'd never go back there again, nor let herself be abandoned. She'd seen that happen to a little boy on the journey out of Sarajevo. As one of the convoys left the city he'd fallen or been pushed from the back of a tractor crowded with refugees. Nobody had stopped for him, so he'd run after, sobbing but still running, holding out his arms to them, begging to be lifted up. She had seen his mouth scream, "Wait! Wait for me!" but nobody had. Daylight had been fading. They were all desperate to reach the safety of the enclave before darkness fell and the shelling began again. Maybe it hadn't even been his family on the tractor. Maybe he'd been lost long before. But whatever it was, nobody had stopped for that kid. He had been left behind.

She remembered looking back at him one last time. He had been standing in the center of the cratered road: a little boy of six or seven, with his mouth wide open and his hair blown back from his white face. Other vehicles had driven round him but had barely slowed down. She had turned away too, unable to watch more, and had hidden her face on her grandfather's shoulder. Recalling the incident now still made her feel dreadful. But it was not going to happen to her. She would not be left behind.

She started across the field. It was like approaching a ski jump in those carefree long-ago days, when there had been school and weekends and holidays in between. Then excitement had made her laugh. She had felt the sharp winter wind rush over her face, and she'd laughed. She had always known that she was going to launch herself off into nothing, had had no choice, anyway, at that speed, but to continue the downward plunge and to jump. Nevertheless, in the moment before her skis left the ground she could never quite believe that she had ever started on the brilliant white incline. Yet she had. And now she took another step across the deserted field.

There was shouting from the road. She crouched down behind the remains of some farming machinery. She must think clearly now and decide what to do. It was no good just running. Even if the trucks did begin to move away she was too far off to reach them in time. Her only chance was to get really close: close enough to smile and to ask.

A car was driven quickly up and down the line. She knew that she must act. Nearby the cat on the top of the wall had woken too. She watched it stretch its back slowly, comfortably. It sat up and scratched, then leaped down and made its neat way through the ruins of the farm. She could make out the tip of its tail as it passed the charred timbers and the piles of tumbled bricks that had once been a house. She could follow its path: at least that way was not mined.

What had her grandfather said? "Choose someone who will do what you want . . . and then ask." That was it. How simple he had made it sound, as though she could have followed the cat across the fields and waved and said "Excuse me . . ." But that wasn't what he'd meant. She understood him now. He, who had survived so much, had known that hope was all that was left for her. The past, within the soft, familiar coverings of everyday life, was gone. It had dropped from her when she stepped from the house. She had shed it just as one of the enchanted creatures in her father's fairy stories shed their old, warm skin to reveal a different creature underneath. It was as if she had slept in an enchanted landscape and had now woken to a new world and an extraordinary forgetfulness that was not unwelcome. She mustn't care about the past. She would let it slip from her like a dark shadow falling into an even darker crevasse in the mountainside. She sensed that if she climbed down after it she might be trapped there forever after.

She glanced round quickly. It was no good: the cat's route was too exposed. It would be safer to go back and follow the stream through the forest. Anyway, if the aid convoy was to be turned back, then it must turn around. It would take time to maneuver vehicles on a narrow road which had probably been mined at its edges. That time would allow her to take the safer route. She crawled backward into the protection of the forest and quickly changed into her one clean shirt and jeans. By the stream she could quench her thirst and wash her face and hands. She could even brush her teeth. It was one of the lessons she had learned during the war: to be helped, you had to look worth helping. If your need is too great, people cannot bear it and they turn away from you. She ate a couple of crackers, zipped up the bag again, and began to make for the stream.

When she was halfway there the engines of the trucks were turned off and a silence settled uneasily over the countryside. Suddenly, every movement within the forest and every step that she took disturbed this temporary covering of silence that had fallen over the valley. She moved as quickly as she could, scrambling through bushes and over piles of debris left by the thaw. By the stream it was cooler. Late violets were in flower on the shaded banks and in the dampest, quietest places, mounds of emerald moss had spread undisturbed. Drops of water glistened on leaf and stone. Ferns were beginning to unfurl their soft pink tips and stretch up toward the sun in a startling brightness of green. Nina was glad and amazed too. She could hardly believe that spring could linger here, quite untouched by war. Yet it did, and she was about to leave it all behind.

She drank quickly from her cupped hand, then splashed water over her face and throat. As she leaned over the water she saw her reflection break, ripple away, and then reform. The face in the water was of a straight-browed, dark-haired girl. Her eyes were light brown: "honey-colored," some people said. Alexander had always teased her and said that she had "yellow cat's eyes." She dipped her comb in and tried to tear through the tangles and make the part neater. It was definitely a serious face and not one of those pretty, "little-girl" faces with upturned noses and cute pink mouths. Her smile was nice, even if a couple of her teeth were crooked. And she would smile. When she asked for help she'd look them in the eye, then toss back her hair and smile her most brilliant, grown-up smile.

She went on, scrambling through debris at the water's edge and slipping on the boulders so that soon her shoes and socks were soaked through. She was making her way nearer and nearer. Sometimes she tried to hold in her panting breath and listen, but it was no good and once when she turned her ankle over she gasped, but there was no one to hear. No one shouted and pointed her out, though she could hear voices now. Up on the bridge above, people were talking.

There were eight, maybe ten vehicles parked end to end along the road: some trucks and vans, a couple of Land Rovers with armor plating welded on to their sides and grills over the windows, and one or two vehicles which seemed to be ordinary family cars, with no protection at all. The first had been stopped halfway across the bridge by the men from the mountains opposite who had set up a roadblock. Some of the vehicles had the emblem of the Red Cross on them and one of the Land Rovers was painted in the colors of the United Nations force. One van only had a sheet tied down over its roof and flapping at the sides. So the information given to her grandfather by the men back at the house was correct. An aid convoy had been expected and had been held up at the bridge.

She was so close that she could see some of the drivers. They were standing around near their vehicles and they looked like foreigners. Three of four of them were leaning over the parapet of the bridge and smoking. No, these definitely weren't local men. She was sure of it. They were too clean and well fed and there was something casual and unreal about the way they just stayed there, staring down into the water below. Didn't they realize that there were snipers hidden up there on the other side of the valley? Snatches of their conversation floated down and she recalled tourists in the lost summers of Sarajevo. They had loitered in the streets in that same casual manner.

Then one of them saw her. He looked away instantly, as though he'd glimpsed something that he shouldn't. Then he glanced back as she hoped he would, and when he did, she smiled up at him with that best and most brilliant smile that she'd always suspected she must have. She didn't move at all, but stood there at the edge of the stream with her bag in her hand and smiled at him. He looked away. She saw his confusion, saw him look past her, look back at the road, lean over and look at the foot of the bridge to see if she was alone, then stealthily, he looked back at her. His gaze slid over her curiously. She waited, pushed her hair from her face with her free hand and heard the silvery sound of the water rushing into the deeper channels beneath the bridge. Then he smiled at her, just a very little bit, as though that was all that she might have.

She felt an extraordinary rush of excitement that was not only fear. Her face burned as though it were on fire. The sweat ran down her back and throat and made her shiver. She saw him bend his head down and scratch his neck, then he turned ever so slightly to the person at his side. He must have spoken because this other man, who wore a flak jacket, glanced over immediately and scrutinized her before turning away with an expression that was closed and final. She knew that he would not help her. "Her" man turned away too, but not before their eyes had met once more.

She took a few careful steps closer, trying to follow bits of the shouted conversations that were being held in English and Serbo-Croat over mobile phones and radios. They were angry and confused clashes. The men shouted the same things again and again before they fell to further swearing. Finally, somebody up there seemed to be giving orders and she saw her man walk away shaking his head as if in disbelief. There were clearly problems on the bridge.

She knew she had to get closer still, close enough for one of them to find something in her face that would make him think of her as an individual and not only as a stranger. And she must do it soon because the light was already changing, yellowing and deepening before it finally began to fade. Surely these men, however inexperienced, would never let themselves be kept here overnight. That would be madness; maybe fatal for them all.

Then, from under the bridge where the stream widened and ran into the river she heard the unmistakable sound of a group of people hurrying along excitedly. Horrified, she tried to retreat, to vanish behind one of the rocky outcrops. Already she was regretting her clean white shirt which was so visible. But it was too late for that. People were approaching the bridge rapidly: an energetic, brightly colored group of women and children with a couple of donkeys and a handcart as well. These weren't refugees on the move again, for they continued to talk loudly, as though they had nothing to fear. Columns of refugees almost always passed by in complete silence. Even their babies didn't cry.

These women called out to the men on the bridge, who replied, and when they did, Nina recognized the local accent: these were people from the mountain villages, the families, probably, of those men who had been up at the house. She crouched down at the side of the water, hugging her knees to her chin, making herself as small as she could, and she began to listen to the bargaining. It was soon clear. These people had been sent by the men who held the mountains above; they offered the safe return of the convoy and its drivers back along the road they had come, in return for some of the aid. She could hear the infuriated embarrassment in the voice of the translator and the strident, brutal need of these women sent down to do business. Of the foreigners' replies she understood nothing. Yet as the sun sank toward the mountaintops and the shadow of the bridge lengthened over her, it was clear that the foreigners were not winning. She heard the doors of the trucks and vans being unlocked and thrown back. Then, when a couple of shells landed half a kilometer down the road, the unloading began. And she was not sorry.

She was beyond caring.

The women were encouraging the animals up the bank on the far side. It was clear that this had been well planned. The boxes and bundles were passed from hand to hand. The foreigners drew apart and watched, then seemed to be involved in an argument among themselves. "Her" man, whom she now recognized again by reddish hair and a beard which were as speckled as a chicken's breast, seemed to be losing his temper. He started toward the women shouting and gesticulating, but a couple of the others ran after him and pulled him back. "Leave it!" they yelled but he threw off their hands and turned angrily away from them all. Then, lighting another cigarette, he looked at Nina again and began to climb down the bank.

Until he was close Nina hadn't thought that he would be so old because he'd moved quickly and jumped the last bit, onto the shingle, but he must have been fifty at least. It was white hair dabbed in with the red that had made him so distinctive. His eyelashes were pale too, and not like anything she'd seen before.

"Here," he said and held a small parcel out toward her. "Here. Take it. If *they* can steal all that, why shouldn't you have this little one. Here."

"I don't want."

"It's all right, really. It'll only be food and clothes. Maybe a toy . . ." He looked a bit uncertain then, as though suddenly aware that she might be too old for toys. "Look. I'll leave it over here. See? You can get it after we're gone. Eh?" He was trying to be kind, fatherly, almost.

She took a step toward him. And smiled.

"I go with? Please?"

She knew she hadn't said it correctly, but she also knew from his face that he had understood her. People must have asked before.

"I'm sorry. It's forbidden."

"Please." She would have touched his hand, if she dared.

"They wouldn't let me!" He jerked his head bitterly toward the men on the road.

"Don't say them. Take me with, please, to England. To Sussex?"

She tried to repeat the foreign word but got confused, so felt in her pocket for the envelope. While he was reading it, something happened up on the bridge. The women were screaming abuse, and banging on the sides of the trucks. Suddenly, from somewhere not so far away, there was the sound of rapid gunfire: one round, then another. A flight of birds flew up from a field. The foreigners were shouting to one another. The engines were switched on and doors were slammed. People were scattering and one of the donkeys brayed before bolting for safety. The foreigners were calling her man. He turned and scrambled back up the bank. When she followed, he shook his head at her, but didn't try to stop her. There was another round of shooting, but not near enough to make her duck. He did. He dropped down on all fours beside one of the great muddy wheels of a truck and she saw terror on his face. There was fallen stuff all along the road and he crawled through it to the last vehicle in the line, then swung himself up into the cab.

When he was safely inside he looked back at her. Then, quite deliberately, he jerked his thumb toward the rear of the truck.

She couldn't reach the handle. She tried again and again, struggling to keep a foot on the bumper, with her body flattened against the doors, but she couldn't manage it, just wasn't tall enough, and slipped back. She fell heavily on her knees on the road, as the truck's reversing lights came on.

6

UNDER BLUE SKY

SHE DIDN'T RECOGNIZE the man who dragged her clear of the reversing vehicle.

"You greedy little thief," he had snarled, his hands under her arms, pulling her roughly to her feet. "Why didn't you stay with the others? Do you want to get yourself killed for a tin of foreign jam?"

Then he recognized her.

"Nina!"

The hydraulic brakes wheezed as the truck began to swing round.

"Nina! Nina Topič!" Slobo repeated. "But . . . Fahro said that they were going to—"

He stopped abruptly. He had let her go and stepped away from her with horror in his eyes as though he could see something dreadful about her, of which she was unaware.

"Slobo? What's the matter? Slobo?"

She could hardly bear to look at him, this young man who had been her brother's friend, who had carried her on his shoulders once. For there were tears in his eyes. She saw his mouth begin to tremble, saw the tears brim over uncontrollably, as he tried to say something he couldn't finish. He was licking the top of his lip, where a purple scar had not healed cleanly. He sniffed and smeared tears and dust across his face like a wretched child. The driver was changing gears laboriously, grinding them, and in that moment, when nothing else moved, Slobo reached over her head, opened the door for her, and pushed her in.

"Go!" he screamed. "Go away, Nina, and don't come back. Ever! Do you hear me? Ever!"

Then he slammed the door and banged twice on the side as the vehicle began to crawl slowly around. Inside in the darkness she staggered, then steadied herself against what seemed to be two huge bales of woolly blankets. Then, little by little, she worked her way between them and crouched down, with her knees pulled up to her chin and her cheek resting on her bag. Eventually she fell into a sort of sleep.

Later, Nina could barely remember details of the journey, except for the oily smell of the blankets and the sudden changes of sound as the vehicle swerved. Those things she did remember, together with her growing hunger and thirst. She knew that they were stopped countless times and searched twice and that she heard more angry confrontations, sometimes from far away but sometimes from right beside the truck. She did nothing at all, just made herself as small as she could and dozed, and when something did wake her, she only burrowed more deeply between the bales, and dragged them together, fraction by fraction, so that she almost closed up the passage behind her. In the end she knew she could not have gotten out at all without help, but it didn't frighten her; not now. She ate the rest of the crackers and the bit of old cheese that was still in the pocket of her pajamas. She drank the water sip by sip and then, when it was all finished and as the hours and maybe days passed by, she gave herself up completely to a listless, sweaty half-sleep that consumed her like a fever.

Sometimes her head ached so badly that she could not think where to rest it and at other times she was woken by pins and needles and then cramps in her legs and arms, but she didn't mind, because every hour of discomfort which passed must, in the end, take her farther away and that was what she wanted. It was all she wanted and she wouldn't have minded particularly if she never reached any other place at all.

She could no longer imagine a destination: she couldn't picture herself "there" at all, taking her place in some other world, walking down some other, unknown street. It was all too difficult and too hard to think about and anyway, she didn't care. Not now. Everything that had been so nice was spoiled beyond repair, and she wanted only to leave it far behind.

Sometimes, as she slipped between wakefulness and sleep, she wouldn't have minded if the convoy had never stopped at all, but had just gone on and on and on, with the darkness and the sour, muddy smell growing stronger and stronger, until it was all too late. Absolutely and forever too late, with the way through the forest not knee deep in red mud, but wiped out altogether . . .

"Hey! What the hell—"

"Good Lord! Just look at this!"

She blinked. They were reaching down, trying to touch her. Someone heaved the bales aside and was touching her legs.

"Is she . . .?"

Someone laid a hand on her neck and she knocked it off and jumped up and was running down the sunny hillside with such extraordinary agility and speed that bystanders pointed and cried, "Look at *her!*" Then she turned to wave and flash them her brilliant, grown-up smile, and she found that she hadn't moved at all. She had only opened her eyes again and been sick when they gave her water to drink.

She took another sip, more slowly, letting it touch her mouth and run down her throat, and then she was able to see their faces, outlined against the dazzling square of light at the back of the truck.

"It's that girl from the bridge!"

And they, surely, were the same two men—the older one with the reddish beard and the other with the flak jacket who was younger and now looked at her with dislike.

"You fool!" he said angrily to the older man. "You stupid old fool! How dare you take a risk like that! Supposing they'd found her! What do you think would have happened to us, let alone to her? How could you put the whole operation at risk like that? You knew it was forbidden!" He was exploding with rage, yet just as suddenly, he quieted down. He squatted beside her, holding a plastic mug steady so that she could drink again.

The older man scratched his neck and shrugged and began to protest that it wasn't his fault: he hadn't *known* that she was in the truck, honestly. He hadn't known for sure. And no harm had been done. Had it?

The younger man turned away, exasperated, shaking his head in bewilderment. He motioned to her to stay where she was and to keep quiet. When he returned he was with a spiky-haired, sharp-faced young woman who began to question Nina, in awkward, strongly accented Serbo-Croat: Who was she? Where was she from? Was she alone?

Nina found it hard to concentrate. Beyond, in that bright square of blue sky, something else that she couldn't quite place kept attracting her attention.

"Your name? You have a name, no? How you say your name?" the woman asked.

And then Nina heard the noise again, heard it tear the blue sky like claws on fragile summer cloth, tearing and tearing, but with the wound healing up behind magically, so that only the memory of the sound remained. There was no scar: no ugly scab of purple on the skin.

"You *must* tell us what your name is," insisted the woman.

"Please, what shall I call you?" The younger man was more persuasive.

"Anja," she said, "you call me Anja."

Nina recognized the call of gulls. They were wheeling on bent white wings in the blue sky, and crying to one another with shrill insistence. It was an unforgettable sound and one that could always be heard, even above the waves, even above the strong waves beneath the ramparts of Dubrovnik. That was where she'd first heard this sound years ago, in her mother's hometown of Dubrovnik.

Surely not. Panic rushed through her. "Are we still . . . in . . ." She got to her feet unsteadily, thought she was going to be sick again, but wasn't. She didn't have the energy even for that. She couldn't bear it, if it had all been in vain and she had not gotten away after all. She didn't understand at first when he said "Trieste." He repeated it. "We are in Trieste. You are in *Italy*, Anja. This is Italy."

She cried then, letting them help her down from the truck and lead her to sit in a small patch of shade, where she shivered with cold though the day was hot and the light impossibly bright. She knew that they were discussing her, although they spoke too rapidly for her to follow. She couldn't concentrate but gazed up at the gulls floating in the blue sky above exactly as they had done before, when she had been some other little girl, holding her mother's hand as they walked along the ramparts of Dubrovnik. Then the gulls had wheeled and cried overhead. Far below at the base of the massive stone walls the waves had broken over the rocks. And she had clung on to her mother's hand.

"Anja," they said, trying not to peer at her too closely. "Anja, how old are you, Anja?"

"Sixteen."

"Sixteen? Really?"

"Oh yes. Definitely, and soon seventeen. But I am . . . too little." She tried another smile; not her beautiful smile: this was her witty smile, the smile of a girl who is almost seventeen and so confident that she can joke about being too short.

The translator, keen to show that she had understood, smiled back at Nina. "Seventeen?" she said. "Really? Peter Gold here tells me that he thinks you want to go to England. That you have an address there." The woman spoke very carefully and slowly.

"Yes. I go to England. To Mr. Fellows." She got out the envelope and pointed to the address.

"He is a friend. He is . . ." She couldn't explain what he was, so she let them do it for her, nodding all the time, at whatever they said, aware that the longer they spent with her, keeping her existence a secret, the more difficult it would become for them ever to disclose it and turn her away.

She held out the envelope with the photos, and they looked at all the bits and pieces, especially the photographs.

"My brother," she explained, pointing to the picture of Alexander on the beach, "my big brother." They looked from the photos to her and she knew they were comparing them, searching for a family resemblance. Strangely, they seemed even more interested in the plane tickets. They examined them, pointing details out to one another. Finally, the younger man leaned over, and gently asked, "Who is Vera?"

"My mother. She is Vera." The unexpectedness of the question had startled her into truth and since it was too late, she went on, "And my father is Georg. Georg Topič." It felt strange; it was a long time since she had spoken their names out loud.

"Where are they now? Do you know?"

She shook her head, and realized what they wanted to ask her, but dared not, so she said it for them suddenly, ashamed of ever having lied to them about her identity.

"They are dead. And Anja, she is dead too."

"No, my dear, don't say that!" They misunderstood her words and refused to accept it. "Don't even think it. You have your whole life before you . . ." The old man was especially indignant. The woman put an awkward arm around Nina and gave her a squeeze rather than a hug. The younger man looked at her with renewed and shrewd interest.

She could not see a way out: explanations were impossibly complicated and although she understood some English, there was very little she could actually say. Anyway, she was too tired. When they asked her about her brother, Alexander, and about other members of her family, she shrugged and said that she had heard nothing for months, or years. When they shook their heads and regarded her with appalled sympathy she was aware of the awful, magnetic simplicity of death. She felt it flowing behind her like the slithering silken train of a princess's dress. Death terrified and excited everyone at the same time. She felt herself to have been set apart, because she had survived.

They took her with them to the small hotel where they were to stay for the night on their way back to England. When she had eaten they left her alone to bathe and then to sleep in one of the neat, clean beds. She slipped her bare feet down between the laundered sheets and then lay back, very still and straight. In the moment before sleep Nina wasn't quite sure if it was her or someone else resting her head on the starched pillowcase.

Outside, beneath the blue sky where gulls still called, she listened to the extraordinarily gentle sounds of a quiet street at midday. People were walking at an even pace, talking and laughing. Cars and buses gurgled and growled around the bends and bumps. She heard a window opened and a woman shouting down to a child. "Marcello!" she cried and then again, but not in panic, or in any sort of terror at all. She was just a mother, calling her child. After a minute, a little piping voice answered, bubbling up like a spring, barely disturbing the lazy movement of the street. Nina turned over and drew her knees up to her chin; at her open window the hotel curtain flapped and fell and quivered in the warm air of the sleepy summer street.

7

WHEN RAIN FALLS

IN THE END, after arguing about every possible alternative, the people from the aid convoy still could not improve upon Nina's original hiding place, between the bales of blankets and other remaining charity goods in the back of Peter's truck. She had sat quietly beside them, watching the drama of the discussion but not understanding it all and not really caring that much. She only wanted to be gone, to be farther away still. All this talk might be strengthening their resolve, but she feared that it would threaten hers. Once or twice she thought of leaving them, of taking her bag from the hotel room and just slipping away from them, letting herself be absorbed into the life of this busy Italian town.

It was not as though she would have been entirely alone. Many other refugees from the former Yugoslavia had also found their way to Trieste, it seemed. She spotted them in the street and overheard snatches of their conversations, but she avoided any contact. She didn't want to be recognized and decided to pretend not to understand if any of them spoke to her, so strong was her desire to escape. She did not want any shadow from the past to fall upon her and its darkness to reveal the person she had once been.

Yet her present companions perplexed her too: they were not like the adults she had known before. Occasionally, Peter Gold, who was "over fifty," as he proudly informed her, reminded her of a history teacher back at school in Sarajevo, but it was really only a similarity of physical type: they shared their age and an extreme, energetic thinness, but that was all. Now, as they sat over dinner in the hotel, Peter Gold scratched his neck nervously and objected to the final plan, which they had all just agreed on.

"Nevertheless," he protested, "I don't think it's right to be underhanded. I still think we should be open about this. We should just say to the authorities, 'Look here, we've found this young orphan girl and we're taking her back to England with us, and—' "

"No, Peter! No!" The woman, who spoke some Serbo-Croat and whose name was Marsha, struggled but failed to keep the impatience out of her voice. "We can't do that, Peter. We've already discussed it."

"I know. I know." He held up his hands as though Marsha were the one causing trouble and he were the peacemaker. "I know all that, but I still want to make my point: that it's not right. Just so you're absolutely clear what my position is! Ethically."

"Don't worry, Peter." Now the younger man, Nick, who had been a soldier, lost his temper again. "Don't you worry: you've made your position absolutely clear! Ethically . . . and . . ." Nick was consumed by his anger and frustration. His face flushed red. He stumbled over his words. "You've done nothing, Peter, nothing but make your 'ethical position' absolutely clear, day in and day out, since we left England! And I've had it up to here with ethical positions!"

They glared at each other across the remains of the meal and once again Nina did not understand why two people who seemed to dislike each other so much stayed in each other's company all the time. As far as she could follow, this aid convoy, of which they formed a small part, had been put together a couple of months ago, in England, in response to the news of the fighting in her country. Individuals and groups had collected donations of clothes and food and medicine and had driven across Europe to distribute these to the people trapped by the fighting and the sieges.

The mission had only been a partial success. There had been accidents and problems all along the route, and after the convoy had arrived in the war zone, things had only gotten worse. They had not been able to go where they had hoped to help. Their disappointment was sharp. It had been a terrifying and confusing experience, and for some reason that Nina could not understand, it seemed that they had not expected it to be like that. Sitting there, listening to them complaining, Nina remembered an evening at the beginning of the war, when she had listened to the grownups in her own family. They had talked like this. They were confused and felt betrayed and were quite unable to believe that their own nation could tear itself apart, slowly cutting limb from limb, in the bloody and fatal surgery of civil war. Only her grandfather, who had fought in the previous war, had predicted what would happen.

Now she heard the same expressions of anger and frustration from these foreigners: why wouldn't the fighters stop their attacks, just for an hour or two, so that they could have delivered their aid and been thanked and then withdrawn hastily, before the killing began again? They spoke as though it was better for people to be killed in foreign clothes and with foreign food in their stomachs . . .

But Nina didn't say that. Oh, no. She took another sip of the wine and reminded herself that she was Anja now, and seventeen, or almost.

The incident on the bridge had been the last straw for the aid workers. Nick spoke particularly bitterly about being held hostage by "a gang of teenage bandits" and "a bunch of greedy peasants." She suspected that he, as an ex-soldier, wouldn't have minded "having it out," as he phrased it, with the soldiers. She suspected, too, that it was frustration more than anything else that had goaded Peter Gold into acknowledging her existence in the first place. He certainly seemed to have lost his earlier enthusiasm for helping her. Now he continually reminded them all of the risks involved in trying to smuggle her into England. She listened, unaffected. It didn't matter, not to her. She didn't care any longer, and especially not about them. And sometimes, as she eagerly ate and drank at their table and accepted the new clothes that they had bought for her, she was surprised by her own calculating indifference. She had never thought of herself as greedy. Times, however, had changed and she was anxious and impatient for whatever she could have.

She had learned that they were waiting here in Italy for the arrival of another vehicle from the convoy which had broken down in Slovenia. When it arrived they would travel back to England together, but Nina's presence was to be kept absolutely secret from the newcomers. They were expected within the next few hours and it was decided that as soon as it was dark Nina was to return to her hiding place in the truck. They had stocked it up with food and drink and some other things which they felt she might need. It was agreed that she should remain hidden until they were safely in England. There she was to ask for political asylum.

"Is this really all right, Anja? Are you quite sure?" asked Marsha anxiously as they watched her climb back in. "You could travel with me . . . if you preferred . . ."

"It is good. It is what I like," Nina replied. And it was true. As she climbed into the stuffy interior of the truck she was not revolted by it, not even by the plastic bucket which Marsha had thoughtfully provided as a toilet. It felt safe inside and when they asked her yet again if she minded whether they locked the doors on the outside, she shook her head. She listened to the bolts slipping into place and to their footsteps drawing away and when she could no longer catch even the sound of their voices outside, she finally relaxed. She stretched her arms out under her head and tried to count the rivets in the ceiling of the truck. Now she could think of . . . nothing; of absolutely nothing at all. She moved her head a little in the palms of her own hands and felt the bands of fear that had been tightened around her stretch just a very little bit. She turned over inside the sleeping bag and drew her knees up to her chin. Outside, the impossible world might scratch at the door but here, for this one moment, she was safe. She curled up very small, and unexpectedly, because she had not even known she was tired, she turned her face eagerly toward the hot, obsessive touch of sleep.

Later she was puzzled to hear her grandfather snoring. She heard her own clear girl's voice tell him to "stop making such an awful row because it will disturb Fahro." Fikret Topič, whose face she couldn't see but whose voice she recognized, remarked that if she thought he was going to change the habits of a lifetime to please a foolish young man like Fahro, then she'd got another think coming! She felt herself puff up with righteous indignation at this unreasonableness in her grandfather. How dare he always know best! Then she tumbled into wakefulness. It was only a dream and no one was snoring, of course. The truck was on the move and the tires rumbled over the roads. She was ashamed of herself and of the treacherous dream-time paths that she must have trodden in the night. If it was night . . .

Peter Gold and Nick had given her a small flashlight and she shone it briefly around the clutter of odds and ends and empty boxes that had not been distributed. Then, remembering how often they had warned her to be careful, very, very careful indeed, she turned it off. She ate some of the chocolate then finished it all off, one piece after another, as though there were somebody else there who might have snatched it out of her hand. Finally, she dozed again, drifting in thick waves of nausea that rocked her gently to and fro. She never found out if it was night or day. Once someone did throw open the doors and look in briefly before closing them up again. Then she waited, desperate to hear the engine turn over, and when it finally did and they were moving steadily on, only then could she stretch out once more and sleep . . .

Once, and for the only time, she tried to imagine how it might actually be, over there, in England. It upset her because she couldn't really picture it at all, so she stopped herself and concentrated on the sounds of the road instead.

"Anja! Anja? Are you all right, Anja?"

It was much later still. She knew that she had lost track of time, and for the moment did not recognize her new name, so did not reply immediately.

"Anja?" There was unexpected concern in Nick's voice. She blinked and saw his outline in the bright block of light that had replaced the door.

"I am all right. I am sleeping." She pushed her hair out of eyes swollen with sleep. Chilled, fresh air was rushing in. She was suddenly aware of how the inside of the truck must smell. And she too. It must be almost as bad as during the siege, but at least then everyone had been in the same position and hadn't washed for weeks. Here it was different. She rubbed her hands over her face and felt miserably dirty and wished that Nick would not come so close, but he did. Now the truck was oppressive in its unexpected silence and quiet. He stood and stared down at her.

"Anja?" He was grinning.

Then she understood.

"We are in England?"

"Yes."

"It is true? I am here? Yes?"

"That's right. You're here!" He was laughing at her, delighted at her pleasure and smiling wholeheartedly, she realized, for almost the first time.

"Come on." He held his hand out. She didn't take it, only stumbled toward the light with a sudden intensity of excitement that made her heart pound. So this was it.

It must be early morning. A wet black road ran past, and along it swished cars, hundreds of cars, with not a mark on them and their paintwork all extraordinarily bright and clean. They went on passing as regularly as a film on a screen. They were in a large parking lot just off the road, with the two vehicles standing side by side. There was no sign of Marsha and her van or of the other people for whom they had waited in Trieste. Peter Gold was there, however, grinning and rubbing his hands together, as though he too found the early morning rather cold. Beyond them, in the rain, the cars flashed over the wet road like flicks of a whip.

There were a few other people about, smart, neat people, in shirts and suits, businesspeople, she guessed, on their way to work. At one side of the parking lot she saw the huge, unbroken windows and the pointed red tiled roof of a new building. Through the plate glass she could see the tables and chairs of a cafeteria. Somewhere, music was playing. Close beside her two women slammed shut the doors of a little green car. They opened up an umbrella and then ran, shoulder to shoulder, toward the shelter of the modern building, splashing themselves and giggling. This wasn't terror and the rat runs of Sarajevo. This was only rain and Nina watched fascinated as they reached the entrance and shook first themselves and then the red and yellow umbrella. When they were ready the glass doors slid open to admit them.

"Well?" Nick was watching her closely.

"Here is England?"

"Oh, yes. No doubt about it. This is England. Look at the rain." He nodded and looked around as though he was as surprised as she was.

When she burst into tears he put an arm around her and suddenly pulled her very close, smothering her tear-stained face. She saw that she had wiped some of her tears onto his blue shirt. When she tried to move away to thank Peter Gold as well, Nick held her back a moment longer. Bending down, he kissed her, half on her hair and half on the back of her neck. Peter Gold kissed her too, then shook her hand vigorously.

"Well," said Nick when they had sat down with their trays at one of the red plastic tables in the cafeteria, "we've done it!"

"We certainly have." Peter Gold startled her by pouring milk into tea and then adding three teaspoonfuls of sugar. He stirred the whole lot round and round so that it looked remarkably like muddy river water. "I knew we could do it. From the moment I saw Anja by that bridge, I just knew that it would all end happily like this!" He took several large and rather noisy gulps. "Now, that's what I call a proper cup of tea. It's the one thing I've never understood about foreigners: they still can't make a decent cup of tea, even after years of Western influence." He grinned at her. "I bet you can't either, young lady! Never mind. You'll soon learn." Then he began to spoon up a large bowl of cereal which swam around in more milk.

"But it hasn't quite 'ended,' has it?" said Nick. He had taken a glistening plate of fried things, sausages and eggs, for his breakfast. Nina, unable to decide for herself, had copied him.

"Not ended?" Peter Gold looked up reproachfully. "What do you mean? I've brought her here safely, haven't I? I've done what I promised I'd do." He folded a triangle of toast into his mouth and started to chew that as well.

"Great!" Nick spoke sharply. "Aren't you a hero! Now what do you propose to do? Let her loose on the highway, like a pet after Christmas?"

"No, of course not. It's just that, well, some of us have taken quite a risk, a personal risk, actually, in carrying out our humanitarian responsibilities to our less fortunate fellow creatures. So I think we're entitled to the satisfaction of knowing that we've done our duty—"

"But that's just *it*. We haven't done our duty. Not yet." Nick waved bacon on the end of his fork.

"I'm sorry, Nick. I disagree. My position, my ethical position—"

"That's rubbish, Peter. And you know it!"

And then they were arguing again. Other customers in the cafeteria turned and stared. Nina sensed that while part of the quarrel was about what to do with her, there were other points of disagreement as well. This, she suspected, was a battle they had fought many times before. She could observe the mutual dislike on their faces but was unable to follow their words. She wished that people wouldn't stare. Then glancing down self-consciously, she was revolted by the dirt ingrained in her hands and by her black-rimmed nails.

"Where is the bathroom?" She had to repeat her question twice before they abandoned their conflict and answered her and even then she knew that it was only a truce.

Nick pointed out the door to the ladies' toilets and she set out across the large space of the cafeteria, walking uncomfortably between the rows of tables. She felt as though every person in the room looked up for a moment and followed her progress with cool curiosity.

She stayed away as long as she dared, doing her best with soap and water and with no comb or toothbrush. She wished that she had brought her bag, but dared not go back for it, not in front of all those watchful strangers. Once she caught the eye of a plump, elderly woman, who also looked tired and disheveled. They smiled at each other wryly. Nina, scrutinizing her own face in this wall of mirrors, was surprised by the thin, pale-skinned little girl whose brown eyes were larger and darker than they had been before. She tried to make her slightly crooked smile more confident and definitely more grown-up as she reminded herself that she was now Anja and almost seventeen. She raked wet fingers through her hair again and bit her lips to chase away some of that pallor.

"On holiday are you?" asked the woman.

"Yes."

"Like it here, do you?"

"Oh, yes. I like very much. Thank you."

"Good." The woman smiled contentedly and Nina understood that from now on she must always like this new country "very much." Yet she hesitated by the door until a family burst in. Little girls were racing each other toward the toilets, and their mother, overburdened with a baby and bags, called to them to stop. Nina held the door open for them all as though this were her country and she was quite at ease. She knew that she must go forward now. There was nothing else to do.

Oh, Anja.

But this was all that was left. She tossed back her hair and stepped out into that no-man's-land of large open space which smelled of burned fat and something too perfumed, and she smiled resolutely in the direction of their table.

Peter Gold and Nick weren't there. She swung round in confusion, then desperation. They weren't anywhere at all. Outside in the parking lot where the van and the truck had been, someone had stood her bag on the corner of a trash can, maybe to keep it out of the puddles.

8

IN QUIET STREETS

NINA HAD BEEN WALKING for an hour at least when she heard the sound of a heavy vehicle pulling up just behind her. She quickened her step. Headlights were reflected in the shine of rainwater on the road beside her but she didn't look back. By now she was soaked and her clothes were beginning to stick to her. The morning rush of traffic had thinned out a little but it was still relentless and she could see that the stretch of pavement was about to end where this road merged with another. She shivered and hesitated. Some of the black mud had flicked up onto her face. It didn't look safe to continue walking with only the gutter between her and the traffic.

She had already passed a couple of small lanes which appeared to run down toward fields and trees but she hadn't taken them. The wet, green landscape had not looked welcoming, and anyway, it had just seemed easier to keep walking straight on. It was not as though she had any idea where she was and it only made her more confused to look continually from side to side of the road. No one had passed her on foot, though several people had turned their heads and looked back at her as they drove by. One or two had even slowed down, she thought, as though they had guessed that she might need help, but no one had stopped, until now. As she grew more and more desperate she felt less able to make any decision. She only knew that she dared not stop walking, not now. It was too late to stop and admit defeat: she had to go on.

Now and then she noticed that the joints at her knees didn't seem to be working properly. She was aware that she was taking one step after another but sometimes she couldn't feel the ground under her feet and stumbled. Then she steadied herself and focused on the ground and went on. She was concentrating so intently that the sudden blast from a horn right beside her struck like a shot.

"Anja! Wait! What do you think you're playing at?" It was Nick, grinning again, as he jumped down from the cab and strode over to her. "Why didn't you wait? Look at you, you silly little thing, you're soaked. Right through."

She pushed back her hair and felt a sly trickle of cold rain run down her neck. He had, she noticed now, extraordinarily pale blue eyes. She was uncertain what to say.

"You shouldn't have run off like that!" It was almost as if he was angry with her, as if she were the one who had done wrong. "Didn't you see my note?"

She shook her head. He began to explain what had happened in loud detail. Peter Gold had been anxious to resume his journey home. He wanted to get back to his wife and family as soon as possible. He was also, Nick insisted, increasingly uneasy about his involvement in anything illegal: as a man of the church he must, he said, be "extra careful." Here, Nick spat dismissively and confessed that in the end he'd gotten so fed up listening to the older man's endless complaints that he'd encouraged Peter to leave. He had even driven in front to show him the best route out of the town. Then, of course, he'd come straight back for Nina. Before getting Peter on his way, he'd written a note and left it on the table telling her to wait for him in the parking lot. She really ought to have read it. He seemed excited and anxious that she believe him. He stood close with his arm around her shoulder as if that might keep off the rain.

"Though maybe," he added, avoiding her eyes, "that note blew away, or someone took it. But I *did* write it, Anja. I promise I did. Did you really think I'd just go off and leave you, all alone, like that?"

She still didn't know what to say because she had panicked. She had never even considered a note or a message. Now she was aware of the warmth of his skin through the wet material.

"Come on, Anja." He shook her, just a very little bit. "Don't be like that, please. Come with me now and I'll look after you. Please? Be a good girl, Anja, eh?"

She didn't understand all the words, but his tone reminded her of something that she did not want to remember. If she hadn't felt so odd, as though her feet weren't flat upon the ground and as though this might all still be a dream, she would not have gone with him. But she did because there was no one else. And anyway this was England: she knew that many things must be different here.

They drove for hours and though she tried to watch for that name Sussex, she never saw it and was relieved when he told her that his home, luckily, was very near Sussex. She smiled at him gratefully then. It would have been so difficult to have found her way this far on her own. He finally stopped outside a house which was small and joined to others on a long gray street. He unlocked the front door and they stepped inside over a tumbled sprawl of letters and newspapers. The house must have been shut up for some time. It startled her to realize that no one had been in it since Nick left. She had assumed that he, too, had a family waiting for him. Now she recognized that smell of neglect. He did not seem to notice anything wrong, but went straight through into a little dingy kitchen and ran the water from the tap until it was no longer brown. There was a plate still on the table, with remnants of food dried as thick and black as tar.

"Well? What do you think?" He seemed to expect her to be amazed, to do something special, or to say something at least, but she just stood in the doorway and looked. It was a poor person's home, narrow and dank and dingy. A red plastic cloth covered a little kitchen table and the walls were darkened by grease and dirt. She hadn't expected this either and felt ashamed for even having noticed it. This man, after all, had helped to keep her alive. A tiny little television perched on a ledge by the stove. He switched it on and she knew that he was waiting for her to be absolutely delighted, so she pretended she was and clapped her hands. He whistled as he ran the cleared water into a kettle for what he called "a nice cuppa." He was happy to be home. Nina recalled some of the housing projects on the outskirts of Sarajevo. They had been cheaply built, like this, but they too had been homes.

"Sit down, then." He pointed to the stool. "Make yourself at home."

"Home?"

"Yes. This is your home now, Anja—"

"No! No!" She rummaged through her bag, searching for the envelope of letters. "My home, it is now Sussex. My grandfather tells me—"

"All right. All right. Calm down. I'll take you to Sussex."

"When? We go now?"

"We can't go now, Anja, it's miles—" He stopped abruptly. "Look here. We're both tired. I'm going out to get us something to eat—then we'll talk. About everything. And don't worry. *I'm* looking after you now. Bye then." He was already taking down his jacket.

"I come too?"

"No. Better not. I don't think anybody should know you're here. Not yet. Not until we've notified the authorities. If they knew you were here, they'd send you straight back, Anja, and you don't want that, do you?"

"No."

"That's a good girl. Now, promise you won't go out. Promise?"

But he couldn't have believed her because when he left he locked the door behind him. She returned to the kitchen and watched the tiny flickering faces on the screen. She did not dare snoop around, though the house was small enough and she could have done it quickly, but for some reason the sight of the steep narrow stairway opposite the front door frightened her. She could not go up it on her own.

The kettle of water began to boil. Through the dirty kitchen window she could see a small back yard fenced around, and beyond it the backs of another long row of drab gray houses. Apart from the television, it was very, very quiet. She smoothed out the letter, and moving her finger slowly from word to word, tried to read it again.

Downlands
Southease
Sussex
22nd September

Dear Vera,

I have not forgotten you and don't think I ever shall. I'm afraid that everyone will tell you that friendships like ours never last. My friends here in England are already saying this, but I don't listen to them and I hope you won't either. Only listen to me: it was the most wonderful summer of my life, in the most beautiful city on earth, and in the company of someone very special.

With all my love,
Paul

P.S. Write soon.

Had her mother "written soon"? Each time Nina read the letter she understood a little more, yet her bewilderment remained. Had those "friends here in England" been right? And had this "Paul" finally listened to them because something *had* happened? The friendship could not have lasted because Nina had never heard her parents speak of it. But it had not ended straightaway, because there was a second letter:

Downlands
Southease
Sussex
4th January

Dear Vera,
I still can't believe what you told me and do not know whether to be happy or sad. It's nearly six months since you first showed me around Dubrovnik, yet it still seems like yesterday—and now this! I think about it all the time. I know that life must be very difficult for you and I'm terribly sorry. I only want to help, so please, please write to me and tell me what you want to do.

Outside it had begun to rain again. The room had darkened and the sky beyond the lines of roofs was low and heavy with a coming storm. What had happened that was so "difficult" for her mother? And had this friend been able to help? If "Sussex" was at all like this, Nina was not surprised that Paul Fellows had fallen in love with Dubrovnik. People always did. It was their Venice: a city of warm golden stone, and little white houses clustering on the hillsides, and wherever you were in Dubrovnik, you could still see the sea, the wonderful glittering Adriatic Sea that curved around the city like a protective arm. Or so it seemed, before the war.

Then her attention was caught by a word she recognized. She looked at the television screen and saw something that was somehow familiar: a young man, in a crowd of men behind a barbed-wire fence, had spoken her own language. He faced the cameras, though some of the other men who were with him had turned aside and were hiding their faces. This man came close, a tall, gaunt man, his shoulders high and stiff and his back bent. His ribs showed through his skin like darkened scars and his mouth—she jumped up and went as near to the screen as she could—his poor, torn mouth with all the teeth knocked out on one side, was speaking her language to a television news crew. There was no doubt. This must be the news about her home, shown here in England. This must be one of the detention camps. They had all heard of them, but she had never seen one until now. So this was where men were being kept before they sometimes disappeared forever. There had been rumors that some of them had been found again, buried in huge shallow graves. When the wolves and stray dogs roamed, neighbors had reported that they pawed at the newly covered-over earth and tried to drag out what they'd found.

Then the pictures vanished. She stood there unable to move until she heard Nick's key in the lock. Then she turned to greet him with immense relief and unexpected pleasure. She couldn't afford to know about things like that, not if she was to carry on. She wanted to forget it all, to leave it so far behind that the path back would be overgrown and it would not be possible to find her way.

Nick was happy to see her welcoming face. He had brought something wrapped up in white paper and now he handed her two parcels that were as soft and warm as a shawl full of kittens. But she could smell that it was food. He made tea, took a bottle of milk from his jacket pocket, and showed her where he kept the plates and cutlery. Then he grinned at her amazement as he unpacked the fish and chips. It was surprisingly nice and she found herself tipping sauce on from a bottle like he did. When she drank her tea she took milk, as he did. By the third cup it was as if she had been doing this all her life.

When the storm hit the house later that night and she woke suddenly, she was unable to remember where she was. She had been dreaming again and this time it was of wolves. One of them had been pawing at the bedroom door. It had stood up on its hind legs, almost like a man. She had heard its breath coming and going as it panted and tried to force its way in. At the moment when it was about to succeed because it had suddenly flattened itself into a shadow which could slip through a crack, at that precise moment, Nina woke. She sat up in the bed and hugged the blankets around her, pushing a corner of the material into her mouth to stop herself from crying out.

Yet nothing in the room had changed. Her shoes and bag, distributed at odd intervals between the door and her bed as her grandfather had taught her, were undisturbed. They were as she had left them, and an old mirror which she had lifted from the wall and balanced against the door handle still rested there. The only sound was from the wind. It drove the rain against the window and, somewhere, out in the night, it swung and banged a door to and then fro, and then again, to and fro.

She glanced out into the night, with its warm orange glow. In Sarajevo, in the war, it had been so dark . . . Here, there were odd lights everywhere. A couple came up the street toward her and the wind blew at their coats. They huddled under an umbrella which swooped and darted from side to side as the wind buffeted it. When they were close she could see that they were young: a man and a woman. Her arm was stretched up over his, and she walked noisily and steadily on red high-heeled shoes and they clung together as though it had been such a great night it didn't matter to them about the storm or the wet wind rushing up the night street. They weren't hurrying. There was nothing to fear in these quiet streets, yet Nina couldn't sleep.

9

OVER THE FENCE

"COOEE! COO-EE! Hey, you there!"

"Pardon me?" At first Nina did not realize that the woman over the fence was shouting at her. She had stayed indoors, as Nick wanted, to begin with. Now sudden sun after so much rain, and her own restlessness, had tempted her out. Dirty puddles lay in the back yard and everything dripped, but occasionally the gray roofs opposite and the sagging black wet fence glittered in the new brightness. She had always heard that England was wet and cold, yet this did not seem like a summer at all.

"Pardon me?" Nina repeated carefully. She had not understood the woman's accent and anyway, Nick had told her not to speak to the neighbors. He hadn't even wanted her to step out of the house. He had said that it wasn't safe for her and that she should avoid it. Today, however, it was too much for her to remain indoors.

"What's your name, love?" This woman was not going to be avoided. She leaned comfortably over the fence, quite indifferent to the wet mark it was leaving on her blouse. She beckoned to Nina with undisguised interest and asked again about her name.

"My name is Anja. An–ja." Nina repeated it slowly. The woman tried it out and then smiled as if she had found it to her liking after all.

"Anja, eh? That's nice. Foreign name is it?" She looked at Nina closely. "Where you from, then?"

"I . . . I am Anja."

"I know *that*, dear. You just told me. So how old are you, then, Anja?"

"Seventeen years."

"No!" The woman laughed at her, but not unpleasantly. "Not you. Never. You don't mean that. You mean something else. Like . . . thirteen? . . . fourteen? You *fourteen* then?"

"Fourteen. Yes. I am fourteen." It was an unexpected relief to tell someone. "But I say I am seventeen. Nick tell me to do this."

"I bet he does! But is that wise, dear?"

"Wise?"

"Anybody can see you're not seventeen. Not you, if you don't mind my saying so." The woman was examining her openly, but with no hostility. "One of my girls is fourteen. That's why I knew you weren't seventeen. So, where you from, Anja?"

"I . . . I have to go. I'm very sorry. Bye-bye."

She hurried back into the house but when she looked through the kitchen window the woman was still there leaning over the fence. She had lit a cigarette and was blowing the smoke up into the air; her pale face was angled up to catch the sun, as though she longed for the summer too. When Nick came in a little later and saw her, he lost his temper.

"Wretched woman! Stupid interfering old cow!" His face and neck were flushed red. "I hope you didn't speak to her!"

"You don't like?"

"Like? I can't stand her! They're a menace, people like that. Lazy gossips the lot of them—sitting at home on their backsides, breeding like rabbits, sticking their noses into other people's business! Parasites they are. You stay away from them, Anja. Do you understand? Stay away! Don't you talk to them or their children. They're just trash. And they'll make trouble—trouble for you and me."

There was no mistaking his anger and she understood enough of his meaning for it to upset and puzzle her. She had always assumed that you needed women like that who knew and discussed everybody's business. How else would you hear of a neighbor's illness or trouble, of a cat lost or a husband's new girlfriend? But maybe it was not like that here, in England. She didn't reply, only stayed indoors for the rest of the day, restlessly moving between her bedroom and the kitchen, and doing nothing in particular.

Nick, who did not seem to go out to work, was almost always at home. He got up late, then spent most of the day in the front room, which he called his office. It was certainly full of office stuff: piles of papers, and letters and reports and dusty office equipment. She could hear him shouting into the phone and the dull, uneven tapping of his fingers on the computer keys, but she couldn't work out what he actually did. When she asked him he only said, "Charity work," and when she asked for details he replied, "Oh, this and that," and grinned at her with his thin lips pressed tightly together. She understood that she was not supposed to question him further, and she began to suspect that he was not really working at all.

He perplexed her. She did not understand how he, who had been so kind to her—*was* so kind to her—could live all alone in this dreary, comfortless house. No one called. No friends banged on the door. No pretty thing had been put in any of the rooms. There weren't even any photographs of family standing on the dusty shelves, just one, of some soldiers in combat dress grouped around a tank. It was pinned up in the kitchen among advertisements for taxi services and take-out Indian restaurants, and other newspaper cuttings that were yellow with age. She examined the photo and then exclaimed with real pleasure when she recognized him among the group. Yet even here he stood slightly apart from the others.

"Mates," he said briefly. "A long time ago." But it didn't look so long ago, because he hadn't changed at all. When she asked him if he still saw these friends he said no. In the long silence that followed he muttered that he didn't have much time for friends and she suddenly wondered about Paul Fellows. What was he really like? Were these English people not good at making friends?

"Tomorrow," she said quietly, "we go to Sussex?"

They were together in the kitchen. He was frying up sausages in a blackened pan and the fat spat noisily. She was smearing margarine on slices of white bread. He ate stacks of it with all his meals. Now she heard him sigh heavily, as though controlling some immense irritation. She saw the back of his neck redden again and she knew instantly that she had annoyed him. He didn't turn round at once and she was glad.

"You don't really want to go to Sussex, Anja. Not now."

"I—"

"Listen to me! Eh?" He swung round to face her, with the cooking fork in his hand. "I didn't want to tell you this, but I can see that I've got to. That you won't let it drop. It's just that I didn't want to hurt you, Anja. Honestly."

"Hurt me?" She had not understood, not completely, and was alarmed. Through the window something caught her eye. The woman over the fence was hanging out washing: struggling with bright orange sheets in a blustery wind. Her hair blew in her eyes and she held some of the pegs in her mouth.

"It's about this Fellows man in Sussex. I've already phoned him. I told him all about you. And . . ." He turned back to the pan and began to prize the sausages apart.

"And?" Nina said eagerly. "Mr. Fellows . . . He waits for me. Yes?"

"No, Anja. He . . . he doesn't want you . . ."

"He does. He wants me. My grandfather tells me that Mr. Fellows helps me—" She couldn't get any more words out. She didn't want to remember.

"I'm sorry. I really am, but it's true." He brought the pan to the table and tipped half the contents onto her plate, half onto his. "Do you understand, Anja?" He was already chewing busily and leaning across the table; he tapped his fork on the edge of her plate to encourage her as though she might not realize that it was food.

"My grandfather say—"

"Your grandfather's wrong!" He spoke impatiently, and she could see a film of sausage fat glistening on his lips. "Anyway, I thought you said your grandfather was dead."

"No!" That was what she had told them. That was what she believed, but she could not bear to hear anyone else say it. "My grandfather is not wrong. Never wrong."

"Okay. Okay." Nick's tone was patronizing. He was humoring her. "But it doesn't change anything. This Fellows guy doesn't want you, Anja."

Nina shook her head vigorously: she didn't want to listen to him.

"I told him all about you," he continued. "I told him your name, Anja, and he said 'So what? What do you expect *me* to do?' Which means, Anja, that he doesn't want you. That he can't help you. And I'm sorry." He spoke the last bit very clearly and much too loudly. Then he put his hand over hers and squeezed her fingers, and she suddenly wondered if he was really sorry at all.

Over the fence Nina could see the washing tugging and flapping in a strengthening wind. She forced herself to eat. She must eat and not think. The sheet flew up in the air and suddenly, helplessly she saw her grandfather's house on the mountainside, as it had been. Her mother had run the clothesline between the cherry trees and when it was windy it had flapped and billowed like sails at sea. When she was tiny she had been so jealous of Anja, who was tall enough to reach up with the clothes and pin them on, whereas she could only hold the basket of clothespins. It hadn't been enough for her. On still summer days the washing had fluttered under the branches like a flight of gentle doves. But in the turbulent storms of spring and autumn, it had blown up in the air and some things had broken free. Then her mother had sent her to find them. That was so typical of her mother: such a good housewife, everyone said; a woman who never wasted a thing, or a word, and was so unlike her father, who would have preferred a world built entirely from the letters of the alphabet. He would have preferred a life of myths and legends, where one story rested upon another and another . . . But not her mother. Not Vera. Vera had no time for make-believe. Unwillingly Nina remembered how she had resented it when her mother made her struggle through the wind and mud after scraps of clothing that were probably already torn and spoiled. "There it is!" her mother would shout and point to something caught on the bushes. She'd wait patiently, with the laundry basket balanced on her hip, until Nina had brought back the lost sock or pillowcase.

"Ice cream?" Nick had large plastic boxes of it in his fridge. It was, he had explained, his favorite dessert, so she ate it too and agreed that it was the best she had ever tasted.

A gust of wind rattled something down the street and more rain slanted against the window. It was almost as dark as winter. Nick wore only T-shirts, but she had felt so cold that he'd lent her one of his sweaters. It almost reached her knees. Tomorrow, he promised gently, he would take her shopping: buy her whatever she needed. So she ate her chocolate ice cream and pushed back her hair. As they smiled at each other across the table she pretended that she had forgotten about Sussex too.

Later she saw the woman from next door reappear in the garden. She was hastily snatching the washing from the line, although it was already wet again.

"I wash up?" Nina offered, because he never did. He left things piled up until there were no plates left.

"No. You don't have to." He always switched on the little television for her before he went into his office.

"I like to, Nick. For you."

"Really?" His voice changed, and he turned excitedly back as if to say something else, but she was piling the dishes into the sink. He hovered for a moment, then, coming close, folded back the sleeves of the sweater for her so that they wouldn't hang into the washing-up water. She found it difficult not to move away. As soon as he had gone and she heard the door of the office close, she turned the tap full on, then slipped out of the back door. The woman was still there, awkwardly unwinding one last thing from the line.

"Please!" Nina cried.

But she didn't hear.

"Help me—"

Their eyes met. The woman looked quickly from Nina to the damp pile of washing in her arms, then slowly she came over to the fence.

"Sussex," gasped Nina. "Where Sussex is? Please?" She shook her head from side to side, trying to flick back the hair that the rain was plastering down over her forehead. She was quite desperate.

"Sussex?" The woman looked surprised.

"Yes. Sussex. You know Sussex? It is . . .?"

"Sussex? That's miles away, dear. You want to go to Sussex?"

"Yes."

"Oh, dear. You're a long way from Sussex here. This is Birmingham!"

"A long way?"

"A *very* long way. Look here—"

But Nina had already run back into the house. A huge mound of foam had piled up over the sink and was beginning to run down. She plunged her hands in and began to wash wildly, letting it splash everywhere. In the other garden the woman had lingered at the fence, then went in too.

So Nick had lied. And she, somehow, had suspected it all along. In the other house over the fence she saw an upstairs light come on. Somebody looked out. Was it that girl, that daughter who was also fourteen? Somebody reached out and drew the curtains, shutting out the storm. Downstairs, the woman, the mother of a girl who didn't need to lie, would be folding up the laundry, finding somewhere to re-hang the sodden things, doing the things that mothers do. Nina couldn't stop herself from crying. She rubbed her hands over her eyes and face, but it was no good, no good at all. She just cried all the more with the foam streaked over her cheeks and the cuffs of the sweater dripping wet.

She had never been sure if she believed his story about Peter Gold, and the note left for her, but there had been nothing else to do. And anyway, hadn't she started it all, back there under the bridge? Hadn't she smiled when she had always been warned not to smile at strangers, not to be too friendly with people she didn't know?

She had only done half the washing up but the water was already cold, with fatty scum around the edge of the sink. She could hear him in the office: tap-tapping away, in little dashes of activity.

"Miles away." That's what the woman had said about Sussex. So maybe Nick had lied about Mr. Fellows too. Maybe he hadn't phoned at all. She peeled off the sweater and dropped it onto the floor before running quickly upstairs. It only took a moment to put her few things back in the bag. She came down more slowly, but he must have heard her or sensed it, at least, because he was standing in front of her, blocking the dark little hallway of his house.

"Don't go." But he wasn't shouting at her, wasn't telling her what to do. He was begging. "Anja. Please."

As though she had anything to give him.

"You don't talk with Fellows!" she cried.

"No. No—I'm sorry, Anja. I meant to talk to him. I was going to, honestly. I'll do it now, straightaway. Only I was afraid—afraid for you—that he wouldn't want you. I didn't want you to be hurt. More hurt. Honestly, Anja, you *have* to believe me. I did it for your sake. I'd do anything for you. It's my whole life, for heaven's sake, doing charity work. I never meant any harm. I just wanted you to be happy—you know, like you were in Italy, after I'd found you. And I know you'd be happy here, Anja. With me. I'll look after you. Anja?"

It was only five steps to the door. She could see the sweat on his forehead, see it staining the underarms of his T-shirt. She could smell his fear.

"Let me take you there, Anja. I can drive you. Please."

She shook her head.

"Come on, Anja, be a good girl. I mean—you can't go on your *own*, can you? You haven't any money!" He tried to laugh, but she wouldn't look at him. She only had to get out of the door.

"Where will you go? Eh? Know the way, do you?" His voice had sharpened but he had stepped away from her. She took off the chain and clicked back the catch.

"Stupid, that's what you are, Anja. Miss High-and-Mighty!"

She opened the door just a very little bit, and edged out into the gusting evening rain.

"Stupid little bitch. Think you can manage your own affairs? Well, go on, then. Try." His voice was rising in fury. "But I'll tell you something else: don't you ever try and come back! Because I won't help you again, you dirty little slut. I won't even open the door."

On the other side of the road somebody had stopped to watch them.

"Go on," Nick yelled, "get lost! And don't ever come back here again. You're all the same, you people. You don't deserve to be helped!"

She looked quickly up and down the street and then, without glancing back, she began to walk rapidly away. She was aware of the person on the other side of the road sniggering at them before he resumed his brief walk home.

10

AS THE WATERS FLOW BY

IT TOOK TWO DAYS for Nina to find her way south and into Sussex and most of another day to get anywhere near the village of Southease.

"Southease?" A woman with a little white dog on a red leash had stopped when Nina approached her. Now she pointed to a path which led away from the small town. "That's it," she said. "That's the footpath to Southease, but it's a long walk." She looked doubtfully at Nina's dirty clothes and the flapping sole of her shoe. "See? That's where it goes." She was showing a narrow track which appeared to follow the full, brown curves of a river. "There's nothing there, when you get to Southease, not even a shop. It's not much more than a cluster of houses. Are you sure that's where you want to go?"

Nina said that it was and took the envelope from her pocket. She had shown it to so many people since leaving Nick's house that now it was creased and the ink smudged.

"Well, it looks as though you're going the right way. And Downlands must be the name of one of the houses." The woman nodded to herself as she examined the address. "Have you come far?" When Nina didn't reply, the woman remarked again that it was a very long walk.

"I like to walk." Nina spoke brightly. It was true, though what she really meant was that she couldn't bear to stand still.

"If you say so . . ." The woman hesitated and was about to say something else but didn't. Then she pointed to the hills in the distance. "We call those the Downs," she said, "the South Downs. The house that you want, this 'Downlands,' must be near there, I suppose." The dog looked up and pulled and whined. The woman laughed. "Well, good luck!" She waved and hurried down the road in another direction. The little white dog scuttled importantly at her side. In the town people were shutting up their shops, putting on their raincoats, looking up at the sky before they hurried home.

It was early evening. Nina climbed over a stile at the roadside and jumped down onto short, springy turf and began to walk along the path. Within minutes the sounds of the small town where she'd spent several hours wandering about had died away. It was very, very quiet. The river slipped in silence between wide, muddy banks. It had been raining here too: the grass was wet and slippery. Before her the river swerved its way in huge curves. Beyond the opposite bank she could see flat meadows, and beyond them, an immense ridge of a green hill which rose toward the sky. And nowhere, among all of this, could she pick out another figure. Nothing moved. Even the sky above was still and gray. She was walking with the current but she wasn't aware of this until she paused to try and fix the loose sole. When she straightened up she noticed a curled feather on the surface of the water. Slowly it floated by. Half an hour later she couldn't even hear traffic on a road.

She hadn't been so alone since she'd hidden in the forest: not so utterly and completely alone. Now she realized that she was not sure how long ago that had taken place. She had tried so hard to keep count of the days but had failed. At least she was certain that two days before she had been in Nick's house; or was it three days now, because already most of this day was gone? Under the burden of the low gray sky that pressed down on the small town, and the shadow of the high green hill, she had wandered up and down streets, playacting the part of a confident girl who was almost seventeen and who wasn't lost at all. Now almost everything was unclear.

Then, as she had hidden on the edge of the forest with the ruined home up on the mountainside behind and the bridge before, even then she had not felt as lonely as she did now. There, she had been surrounded by ghosts and she had had some knowledge of the patterns of their lives before all was ripped up and scattered by war. The presence of those who had died had been as powerful to her as the smell of rain on hot summer earth. Out here there was nothing of that: here nothing belonged to her at all.

The silent swing of the water and the smooth green hills were not hers. Her steps, soundless and printless in the grass, would be unseen. Looking back, she saw that she had left no trace. She was again troubled by the sensation that she was not really walking at all. She could have been floating on the surface of the river, being carried inconsequentially along and never even glancing down at the mud which oozed and shifted below.

Then she fell. She had reached a part of the path where the grass had been worn away. The soil beneath wasn't ordinary mud but was gray and not earth at all. It was more like rock, and as slippery and treacherous as ice, after the rain. When she got to her feet she saw that the sole of her shoe had come off completely and there were streaks of white all over her jeans. It covered the palms of her hands, but when she tried to wipe it off, it stuck and became engrained. When she stood up her head was unsteady on her shoulders and the green hill tipped ever so slowly to one side.

The truck driver who had brought her south had bought her lunch in a café on a highway. He had also given her some money. It was a small brown bill which she'd folded up and put in her pocket but hadn't dared spend. She didn't know what it was worth and was afraid to go into a shop in case people laughed or, worse still, suspected her of trying to cheat them. She had seen that happen in Sarajevo. A young foreign woman, a journalist probably, had tried to buy milk with a worthless bill that wouldn't have bought a single drop. Bystanders had been unpleasant to her. They had shouted at her to go back where she belonged. Why, they said, was she trying to cheat them of what little they had? Nina, who had been waiting in the line too, had seen that it had been a mistake. The foreigner had only been confused. Now, as Nina touched the corner of the folded bill, she knew that she did not dare try and spend it. Luckily she wasn't hungry any longer. This morning she had been starving and thought of food endlessly. Now the thought of it revolted her. She was thirsty but that was because she felt so hot. She suspected that she'd caught a cold, if not flu. It was hardly surprising after being out in so much rain. Yes, her cheeks felt distinctly flushed. There was a roaring sensation in her ears. It blotted out all other sounds, even her own footsteps. Maybe that was why it was hard to keep her balance. Maybe that was why she had fallen over, that and the shoes. She had never liked them; her grandfather had brought them back during the siege. They were worn out before she got them. Now the stitching had burst open so that her sock was soaked and her toes were numb with cold. Her fingers were cold too. She glanced down at them and at her hands smeared with the gray mud from underfoot.

Oh, Anja.

Suddenly, unwillingly and in the shadow of the hill, she remembered the day of the hail in spring. They had gone back into the warm house, leaving their muddy shoes at the door. As they sat by the stove in the kitchen, getting in their mothers' way again, she'd picked the remaining blossoms from Anja's long dark hair. And after the hail, the sun had come out, brighter than before, but her grandfather had shaken his head at them all. The crop wouldn't be very good that year . . .

"Oh, Anja . . ."

"Pardon?" Someone had answered her.

She gasped in fear and swung around. A tall man with untidy gray hair was only a stride away. Had he been following her?

"I'm sorry," he said, and put out a hand, as though he, too, would have touched her. She flinched. "I'm *so* sorry. I didn't mean to startle you. I thought you'd heard me coming, I thought that you said something—"

She didn't reply. He'd noticed her broken shoe and looked away. She stepped off the path into the muddier edges near the water. She wanted him to go, to walk away and leave her alone with her misery. He hesitated. She knew he was still there but she didn't turn round. The river must have been even fuller a few days before. She was standing in a wavering flood mark of rubbish left by the receding waters: muddied packages and plastic things; bits of sodden black wood and the pale pink up-turned shells of little crabs.

"You did say something, didn't you?" he tried again. "Can I—"

"No!" she shouted, but with her back still to him. "No!"

"Okay. I'm sorry. I'm *really* sorry—"

"Go away from me!"

"Yes. Yes, of course." He left her then, almost running in his eagerness to escape. Was he relieved to have gotten away from such a pitiful creature?

Down at the water's edge the gray rock had been smoothed away and covered with mud and slime. The water was opaque. She could not see into it at all. If she had slipped, after the first moments of terror there would have been no trace. No trace at all, and nobody to know.

Maybe Nick had been right and it was all that someone like her was fit for. And it hadn't only been Nick's opinion. After leaving his house she had walked into town and spent the first night at a railway station. She had come upon it by chance and it immediately reminded her of the main station in Sarajevo. Even before the war it had always been full of people who had nowhere better to go: drunks and drug pushers mingled with illegal immigrants from Romania and Bulgaria. Poor people of all sorts were mixed up with tourists and travelers and local people just going about their everyday lives. Stations were impersonal places where nobody, among the coming and goings of trains, was at home. They were places to kill time in and places where one wasn't noticed.

At first she pretended to be waiting for a train and anxiously examined timetables she didn't understand. Then she wandered from one corner to another, trying to look casual and bored at the same time, as though she might have been waiting to meet somebody who was very, very late. Finally, she just sat . . . She had been amazed to see people actually begging for money. Some were very young. One, a girl of her own age perhaps, was seated on a folded sleeping bag near the entrance. A message written on a piece of torn-off cardboard was propped up beside her. She didn't move but repeated something over and over again to all the passersby. Some dropped a coin or two into her outstretched hand. Most walked past as though they were quite used to seeing her there. Nina had stared in astonishment. The girl told her to "piss off." She didn't understand, and when she didn't move on, an older man stepped from the shadows of an archway.

"You stupid or something?" he snarled. "Didn't you hear what my girlfriend said? This is *our* pitch. So get lost, darling."

"Please . . . I—"

"Don't make me say it again: just go away! Go and spoil

somebody else's day!" He laughed then as though quite pleased at his own wit.

"Please. I only am liking—"

"You foreign or something?" He had a fat face and almost no hair at all, just a gray stain over the top and back of his head, which had been shaved. Wrinkles of plump, pink flesh at the back of his neck pressed against the collar of his black leather jacket. He didn't look hungry at all.

"See her?" he remarked loudly to no one in particular, but jerking his chin at Nina. "Look at this bloody foreigner coming here to steal the jobs we haven't got!" He laughed again and a few of the people who had turned to watch sniggered in agreement. One, a smart young man in a suit, pulled a face of mock horror when he looked at Nina. Then he brandished his umbrella at her as though she were some dangerous creature. As she crept away, one loud, self-satisfied woman's voice rose above the rest: "Disgusting, I call it! This is what happens when you let these foreigners come over here! They put their children out to beg! Disgusting, that's what it is. We should send them back, back where they come from!"

Nina had felt disgusted too, not just by the woman. She was disgusted with herself for needing help and for taking it. She had seized whatever had been offered to her. She was no different from these beggars; she might not have held out her hand, not yet, but maybe that was only a matter of time.

As she hesitated, an elderly man and woman stepped toward her, against the flow of the crowd. She knew that they wanted to help, that they had recognized her desperation, and suddenly, bitterly, she couldn't bear it. She avoided them and darted away, leaving the station immediately and spending the rest of that night hiding in a little hut in a park close by. As soon as it was light she had found her way to a main road and begun to hitch a ride, asking for Sussex and Southease. At first she was not even going in the right direction and she was certain that she couldn't have gotten here at all without the help of Chris, the truck driver who had picked her up later that morning. He had taken out his map and found Sussex and then Southease. They had traveled down to London, where he had passed her on to a friend at a truck stop. He had given instructions that she was to be helped on her way. But even Chris had not thought well of her. His daughter, he said, would never have been allowed to hitch and wouldn't have wanted to either. He'd guessed that she was in trouble, but when she wouldn't answer his questions he'd looked at her doubtfully and she knew that he was hurt that she wouldn't trust him.

For most of the journey she had no idea where she was and only realized gradually how far Nick had taken her from the place where she wanted to be.

"Ask," her grandfather had advised her. "Choose someone who will say yes, and then ask for what you want."

How could he have said that to her? Hadn't he considered the cost of asking? Hadn't he realized that it would lead, inevitably, to this, where she must beg and where everything was muddied beyond repair? Had he never thought that a time would come when she would be too tired to even smile?

Then she saw a stick float past her—but it was going the wrong way, if the current of the river had changed. Yet that couldn't be. Idly, she picked a frond of green leaves from a muddy clump nearby, and tossed it in. It spun round and round and she watched the bright rings eddy outward. Then it began to move. Intrigued, she climbed back onto the path. Without any doubt at all, the leaves were being carried back toward the town she had left behind. Had she been mistaken, then, about the direction in which the river flowed? Looking ahead, she saw that there seemed to be something in the distance spanning the water. She began to walk more quickly. It was a narrow iron bridge, painted green. From there she could easily tell which way this river flowed.

Years ago, before the war, before the landslide had carried it away, there had been a simple bridge over the mountain stream at home. She and Anja had often played there. Lying side by side on the warm wooden planks, they had reached out, shoulder to shoulder so that at exactly the same moment they let go of their sticks. Then they'd raced to the other side to see whose was carried down first. Anja's long black hair had hung down, touching the water sometimes, and when she'd sat up, she'd tossed back its dripping ends and splashed them both. They'd laughed so much, rolling about bare-legged on the warm, worn planks of the bridge, that they'd forgotten whose stick was whose. They were always laughing. They'd choked with laughter about absolutely nothing at all . . .

Now, as she climbed wearily onto the bridge, she saw houses through the trees. The woman with the little white dog had been right. This was hardly a village, just a cluster of houses. And there was no one about.

Forgetting all about the river, she began to hurry along the lane. There was a tiny church opposite with a graveyard around it and a seat by the wall. She sat down and took out the letter. There was no doubt at all. A sign in black and white read "Southease," and on the gate of the house beside the church, the name "Downlands" was carved.

Then, from behind her, she heard voices. A man and a woman were talking quietly in the garden of the house beside the church. Instantly, and not knowing why she did it, Nina ran into the churchyard and crouched down behind the wall. The couple passed quite close, just on the other side. A gate clicked. Peeping over, she saw an elderly woman walk across the yard to a cottage on the other side. The man went back into his garden and after a moment she heard the snip and scrape of garden tools as he resumed some work.

It was the man who had spoken to her down by the river. She recognized his long gray hair. He was cutting back plants which had overgrown a path at the side of the house. For some reason that she did not understand, she was certain that he was Paul Fellows.

11

FROM BESIDE THE GRAVE

HE WORKED on in his garden as the shadows lengthened and evening became night. Nina watched. She had found a place at the back of the churchyard, where two yew trees grew close together. From there she could see him yet be unseen herself. A stripy orange cat with a face that was half white and half orange followed him around and mewed. It sprang from a window ledge and rubbed against his ankles. He picked it up and cradled it in his arms. She heard him talking to it for a moment before he set it gently down.

Watching him secretly from among the dry, black dust of old trees, she longed to jump up and run up to him, shouting, "It's me, Nina: I'm Vera and Georg Topič's daughter!" She pictured a kind expression of growing amazement, then recognition, on his face. He would put aside his work, be astounded that she had arrived safely. He would want to know everything about her and they would like and understand each other at once. Her desire was so intense that she could almost believe she had seen him somewhere before and that he wasn't a stranger after all.

Yet she remained hidden, tortured by the fact that down by the river she had driven him away and rejected his offer of help. And it was not that alone which held her back. Nick's words remained with her. He had certainly lied to her, but what he said could have been true: maybe Paul Fellows would not want to have anything to do with her. Maybe, when she smiled and asked for help, he would say no, and shut the door in her face.

Finally it was too dark to see. He had piled the cut branches onto a wheelbarrow and as he pushed it toward the end of the garden the wheel squeaked round and round. She heard the sound of a brush driven swiftly down the path; in another moment he would go in. He could do no more and it would be too late. There were no stars in this sky but occasionally the clouds parted to reveal a moon hung above the spire of the church. And there was still no sound at all. No car drove by, no children played a last game, and no one leaned from a window to call them in.

Then a phone rang. She heard him drop the broom down and run in muttering, "I'm coming," as the phone rang again and again. He had put a light on. Moving closer, she saw him inside the house talking, saw the cat jump up near him. Now was her chance; when he came out again, to pick up the broom and put away the tools, she must approach him. But he didn't come out and when she crouched down and rested her head against the wall in despair, she must have fallen asleep.

Later, it was so cold in the night that she woke and put on all the clothes she had, including her grandmother's jacket, but still could not stop herself from shivering. She swung her arms and paced back and forth.

When the moon shone briefly she walked to the church and tried the door but it was shut. In the house no lights burned, and she would have gone back to her place behind the yew trees if the little cat had not suddenly appeared on the wall. She saw its eyes first. Then it paced along, putting one paw in front of the other, and Nina followed it out of the churchyard. She opened the gate to Downlands and shut it again without making a sound, then felt her way down the garden path. She knocked against the broom but no one heard. The cat stopped outside a shed at the end of the garden and rubbed its face against Nina's feet. She put out her hand and touched a hinge, then sliding her fingers across she found the edge of the door and then the latch, which seemed to be only a nail, bent round. The cat pushed confidently past her as soon as the door was open, as though it knew where it was going. In the darkness she heard it spring up and land, scratch a little and begin to purr. Then she saw its yellow eyes again, quite close. She pulled the door shut, felt her way over the floor, and slowly and cautiously crawled onto something that was smooth and soft and very nearly warm. She drew her knees up to her chin, stroked the cat's head, and settled herself more comfortably.

She half-woke later and was aware of something heavy pressing her down. Imagining that she was back in the aid truck and that one of the bundles had shifted slightly, she felt around, pulled at a handful of cloth so that she could stretch out more comfortably, and drifted straight back to sleep. Then she woke again. It was still dark but the pressure on her ankles was unmistakable. Sweat was trickling down her stomach, moistening the backs of her knees, although she felt intensely cold. This time there was no doubt: she knew where she was. The tall man with the cross at the neck of his shirt was sprawled over her ankles, pinning her down and hurting her so much. Once again he didn't care about her pain and once again she was paralyzed and unable to do anything at all. She struggled to move without revealing her hiding place and to scream for help, but when she did she could not be heard. She screamed and screamed but made no sound at all. And all the time that her cries were unheard she could hear the rough sound of flesh on flesh. He was rubbing the palms of his dry, red hands together. He did it again and again and again and she could do nothing at all, neither move nor make the very faintest sound.

The chair overturned. It fell back onto the veranda floor and Nina, dropping headlong into wakefulness, saw that the orange cat had jumped from its place on her feet onto a table beside the sofa where she had slept. It had knocked off a mug and a book. Now, without a care in the world, it continued its meticulous grooming. Stretching out a back leg, it licked and licked with its rough, pointed tongue. Nina, propping herself up on one elbow, let go the breath she had been holding in and felt the nightmare slowly recede.

She was not in a toolshed, as she had expected, but in some sort of studio. There were pictures pinned up everywhere and the shelves around the walls were stacked with hundreds of boxes of photographs, dog-eared files, and spools of film.

There were books and papers and carvings and pieces of rock and pink-mouthed shells from faraway warm seas. Mixed up with these were objects left over from everyday life: some cans of food, an iron with a chipped handle and a pile of odd socks in a plastic bowl, another mug and plate, and a vase of flowers that had dried up. Everything was covered in dust and a spider had attached part of its web to the corner of the sofa where she lay.

She righted the mug and the book. It did not look as though anyone came in here very often, apart from the cat, which now strutted over to the door and mewed for her to let it out.

She did so, opening the door a tiny bit, expecting all the time that someone would notice and call out.

She turned the stiff tap over the sink and drank from it, sip by sip, and dipped her finger into a bowl that was, as she hoped, full of sugar. It was not bright in the room because the windows were overgrown. Looking out through the tangle of leaves and thorns and rosebuds just touched with crimson at the edge, she imagined she heard her father's voice. Once, long ago, she had been ill. It was flu or a cold or something wintry, and she had been small and very miserable. Unusually, her father had been left in charge of her and neither of them was enjoying it. He had been exasperated by her unreasonable demands that he somehow bring her mother home at once. In the end when she had refused everything else, he had brought in a book and begun to read. When she'd cried louder still, working herself up to near hysteria, he'd kept on reading, raising his voice too; he was as relentless as the fairy stories themselves, in their headlong plunge from misfortune to tragedy.

But he'd won. She had been silenced by the deluge of his words. Her tears had dried, and reluctantly she had begun to listen. They had been foreign fairy tales and he had read right through the book, hardly bothering to draw breath, as long as she kept quiet. He had unfolded the tales like scarves shaken out in the sun: the ugly duckling, the princess and the pea, and then the wolf who ate the seven little kids; then Rumpelstiltskin, then Rapunzel, and then, near the end, the story of Sleeping Beauty, which she had never liked. He had been wearing his brown and white jacket, which was old even then and such a disgrace that her mother wouldn't let him wear it outside the house. She had already stitched leather patches onto the elbows and around the cuffs. He had been leaning comfortably back in a chair with his long legs propped on the side of her bed, even though she'd tried to push his feet off, at first. He'd sighed, not so much in anger as in surprise that she didn't love these stories as much as he did. But she'd listened, that day, to his fantasies of princesses whose windows were barred by roses and thorns.

He had worn the same jacket the day they took him for questioning, although it was even more dilapidated by then. It had been a Saturday morning. The bell had rung. When her mother opened the door the superintendent from their apartment building and other neighbors whom they knew, who were all in uniform, pushed their way in. Her father had got up to meet them with a book in his hand. When he heard what they wanted he went back for his briefcase and his jacket. Her mother had protested, getting between them, pushing them away, pulling him back into the apartment, but it hadn't done any good. A neighbor opposite, who had recently moved into an abandoned apartment, had stood in the stairwell and watched.

The professor would be back soon, explained the superintendent, not looking them in the eye, but there were some questions to be answered about his research.

She had watched her father walk down the street toward the waiting truck, wearing his jacket and with his briefcase awkwardly under his arm. His book was still open in his hand as though he intended, somehow, to carry on reading.

She had always despised his princesses who waited patiently behind high walls and thickets of wild rose. Why didn't they climb out? she had always asked him mockingly. That's what she would have done.

Now, suddenly, she was no longer so sure. She glanced round again with indifference and no curiosity at all. She lay down on the sofa, not even bothering to cover herself with a rug that was nearby. She longed only for sleep that would be undisturbed for a thousand years.

"What the hell are you doing here?" He was standing over her, carrying a large box piled high with papers. "Well?"

"I'm Nina." Then she said it again and remembered to smile, but he didn't seem to understand. "I'm Vera and Georg Topič's daughter. From—"

"Vera?" Some of the papers tipped, then tumbled off onto the floor, but he didn't move. He didn't take his eyes from her face.

"No. Not Vera," she tried to explain. "I am Nina."

The look of recognition in his face faded and she wondered if she should have smiled more, but she was too tired.

"Who are you?" he asked, more gently.

Very slowly she moved her hand toward her bag. She had extraordinary trouble opening it. He rested the edge of the box on the table, watching her closely.

She found the packet of letters and the photos and held it out. His hand was unsteady as he took them from her. He put down the box, then turned the letters over one by one, just as if he'd never seen them before.

"You come from Dubrovnik?"

"No!"

"Who sent you here?"

"My grandfather. He sends me here."

"Then where did you find these?"

"Here." She pointed to the jacket pocket where they had lain hidden all these years, but he didn't understand.

He shook his head from side to side in disbelief and she could not begin to explain. Drawing on the remains of her courage, she pushed her hair out of her eyes and looked up at him, willing him to like her, just a very little bit. When he stared at her with the same expression of disbelief, she pointed to the photo of Alexander on the beach in Dubrovnik.

"He is my brother," she whispered. Maybe this man would like her brother's face more. "This is Alexander."

"No." His voice was sharp.

"Yes. Alexander, he is my oldest brother. And—" She wanted to explain that he was her favorite.

She remembered Alexander's smile. She saw him reach down for her as he had so often done when she was just a little girl. He used to pick her up in huge, firm hands and toss her shrieking and laughing into the air. He had turned her upside down and swung her round and round, and always, just at the last moment, when she thought that she would never be able to stop laughing, he had cradled her in his arms before setting her safely down on her feet. She had begged for more, and pulled at his hands and shirt, unable to understand why such happiness should ever be ended.

"It isn't Alexander," he said unsteadily.

"It *is!* It *is!*" She hated this man who refused to understand, with a sudden energy that made her snatch the photo out of his hand.

"He is my brother and you . . . you do not know. You do not know about us, about anything."

How could he, in this quiet house, behind this quiet, green hill? How could she ever have been such a fool? How could she have expected anything from this man whom her mother and father had not trusted? If he had been even a half-decent person her parents would have remained friendly with him. She would have heard about him. Her father, who was so absent-minded, might not have kept in touch, but her mother would have. Before the war Vera had exchanged letters and New Year cards with other people she had known in her student days in Dubrovnik and who were now scattered around the world. No card, however, had ever come from England.

She saw her mother's face with cruel, unwelcome clarity: her straight, dark brows, her peaceful, slanting eyes. She had been the quiet one in a family of talkers, patient and practical while others dreamed. She had been a secretary in the hospital before the war and had kept going in to work, risking her life each day, until the siege finally made it impossible. She had always been a good housewife and their home had run like clockwork. The fridge had been full of her amazing food, the house had been bright with her care. Nina was sure that that was partly why her father-in-law, Fikret Topič, had loved her so much: she was so competent and so sensible. She was the best thing that had happened to his son, he always said. Even during the siege, she had kept them from starving and freezing. She had made something for them, out of nothing at all.

On that day, when another ceasefire had been agreed on and the shelling had stopped, people came out of their houses again. Vera had gone to line up for water. She had just filled one can when a single shell came down among the crowd. When the stretcher bearers could reach the wounded hours later, they had found Vera propped up against a wall. She must have crawled there. She had cradled the precious container in her arms while she bled to death. Most of the water, they said, was unspilled. Her grandfather hadn't let Nina go to her mother's funeral. It was too dangerous: the snipers up on Mount Ignam targeted mourners. And what was the point? Yet she would have liked to have seen the grave. Neighbors told her that it was really quite nice: it was in part of what used to be the park. Nina believed them but she would have liked to have seen it, for herself.

Soon after her mother's death her grandfather had taken her away and now . . . now she had come to a man whom her mother had chosen to forget.

She looked at his thin frame, his straggling gray hair, his anxious blue eyes, and at this studio that spoke only of neglect, and she did not like him at all. Why, even Nick had shown more warmth and emotion; Nick had wanted her to stay with him, whereas this man, this Paul Fellows, was clearly just an idiot.

"It *is* Alexander," she said, scowling, and pointed to the photo stubbornly. "He's my brother and he is now twenty-seven."

"No, it isn't," Paul Fellows said quietly. "It's me."

12

DOWNLANDS

WHEN NINA WOKE again, blue-and-white checked curtains were drawn across a small window. They barely held back the light of some brilliant day and to begin with she lay still and stared at the fans of sunshine on the wall. She was in a small, white-walled room. Somebody had put marigolds in a little yellow jug on top of a chest of drawers. One flower had opened wide and petals and pollen lay on the polished wood as bright as gold dust. How long, then, had she slept here, and fully dressed like this? There was a rug by the bed and a wicker chair with a cushion near the window. At least she wasn't wearing her shoes. They, or what was left of them, had been neatly placed, side by side, on her bag.

She got out of bed slowly and unsteadily as if she had been ill. The soles of her feet hurt. There was a half-empty cup on the bedside table. Had she drunk that? She parted the curtains and was surprised anew. She had expected the devastation of the landslide, not the quiet curves of a river beyond the trees, or those smooth, green hills. From up here they seemed to stretch forever, like cupped hands laid one upon the other, as far as she could see.

There was the churchyard on the left. So there was no doubt: she was in his house, in Downlands. Had he taken her up to this room? Had he brought in that cup? If he had, she wasn't pleased. She remembered what he'd said and she was angry with him even if it was a joke. But she was more furious with herself for coming here at all.

She opened the bedroom door. No one was about.

Along the landing she found a bathroom. When she washed her face and hands the dirt ran black in the basin and she was too ashamed to use one of the towels. The face that looked back from the mirror was no longer hers. It was years older than Anja had ever been, and hardened too, with lines on her forehead that hadn't been there before. There would be no need to pretend to be a glamorous seventeen-year-old. She wouldn't be turning many heads and if she did, it would only be because of pity or disgust.

At the top of the stairs she hesitated. Kitchen sounds floated up from below: music was playing quietly and plates were being moved about. A kettle had been left to boil too long, then was poured. She smelled coffee suddenly and her mouth watered. She was back on the street at home. In Nick's house they had drunk something he called coffee but it hadn't smelled like this. It hadn't actually smelled of anything at all. This was as it had been, surely? There had been a coffeehouse on the square in Sarajevo. She used to pass it on the way to school, but had always begun to notice the scent of roasted beans a couple of streets away. As soon as it was warm enough, students had sat at tables outside. She would have sat there, with Anja. They would have sipped their coffee and watched the world stroll by and sometimes, for a treat, had chocolate cake as well. Slowly, step by step, she came down the stairs.

Paul Fellows stood at the sink pretending, she suspected, to wash up. That way he could avoid talking to her, because he must have known that she was there, at the kitchen door. He didn't greet her. He didn't even turn round. She was determined not to care. Anyway, it gave her more time to look about. A door into the garden was open and she could see the shadows of leaves and hear the hum of bees. The cat sat neatly in a square of sunlight on the red tiled floor, and on the kitchen table were the coffeepot and a mug and plate.

"Well," he said at last, drying his hands, "did you sleep well?"

"Yes."

"Would you like some coffee?" He took another mug and asked her about milk and sugar as though this was what they did every day. "And bread?" When she nodded he cut a couple more slices and got out butter and jam. She guessed that he was trying not to look at her too closely. He asked her if she liked animals and then if she liked his cat. It was called Kitty.

"Yes," she said. "I like the animals."

But then a silence settled heavily between them like an unwelcome guest. Paul Fellows poured himself more coffee and flipped through the pages of a newspaper too quickly. She knew that he wished she had never arrived to disturb the peace of this quiet, sunny morning.

She also suspected that he lived by himself. There was no litter of other people's shoes by the door, no sweaters flung over the backs of chairs. He had stood a single mug and plate and a small saucepan on the draining board. There was no family here. When he seemed to be occupied reading the newspaper she examined his thin-lipped face, his horrible lank hair, and his free hand tapping the table. It wasn't loud but it was incessant. He was impatient. He didn't want to sit here and he didn't care if she knew. If she had had shoes and if her feet weren't so blistered she could have walked off: eaten a few more slices of bread and asked for some money, or taken it maybe, if the chance arose, then gone on to somewhere else. Maybe she could hang about for a few more days, and still move on. This man wouldn't care. He'd be relieved.

"About that photo," he began.

"Of Alexander?" Her voice was quick and sharp.

This time he didn't contradict her but just sighed and turned the pages of the newspaper again. Then, without looking at her, he asked if she'd like a shower. He had, he said, some clothes.

"*Clean* clothes," he emphasized. He took some children's garments from a plastic bag at his feet. He dangled pajamas with racing cars or something like that on them and a faded red sweatshirt. They were used things and he seemed to expect her to be delighted.

Nina could have spat at him but followed sullenly as he pointed out which tap was hot and which cold and how to close the door. Then he demonstrated which bottle contained shampoo and which bath soap. He brought a large, fresh towel. She scowled. Did he think she was stupid or just a peasant who had always drawn water from a well? She slammed the bolt across the door as soon as he was outside and turned the water full on. In moments the room was full of steam. She peeled off her clothes and, letting the water run as hot as she could bear, stepped underneath so that it streamed down on top of her.

She didn't take any notice when someone began banging on the door and rattling the lock. She had washed her hair several times with half the shampoo in the bottle and was enjoying the dance of the water on her closed eyelids when someone shouted her name. She tried to turn off the tap, deluged herself in cold water then scalding hot then cold again, and as he yelled she made a grab for the towel and stepped out onto the flooded bathroom floor. Even the carpet on the landing outside was soaked through and the water had begun to drip down the stairs.

"It'll dry." He sighed, opening a window and letting in a rush of cool air. She knew he was annoyed. He showed her again how to angle the jet of water and shut the shower door. Then he was down on his hands and knees trying to mop up with towels and sponges. She dressed reluctantly in the borrowed clothes, then stood around getting in his way, not able to help, but not really caring at all.

"Well," he said when it was finished, "that's not too bad, is it? Are you happy with your new clothes?"

"Happy?" She did not understand.

"Do you like the clothes?" He spoke too slowly and too loudly.

"Yes. I like the clothes." She detested them and suspected that they weren't girls' things at all. The same name was on a small label sewn onto each of them: David Adams. Even she could guess that this was the name of some English boy.

Later, they ate a meal on opposite sides of the kitchen table and Paul Fellows still did not ask her anything. She did not understand how anyone could be so indifferent or so lacking in curiosity. But maybe this was how people behaved in this country. If it was, she realized that she must now follow his example, so she didn't ask him anything and they ate in almost total silence. If the cat had not jumped up onto the table and tried to steal something from her plate they might have said nothing at all.

When Nina knocked the cat away Paul Fellows looked up in surprise and, calling it back, settled it on his lap and fed it with scraps from his plate. She was so revolted that she could barely continue to eat. In her mother's kitchen nothing like that would ever have happened, and she watched in disgust as the cat licked the grease from its paws.

During that first week Nina felt as if she and Paul Fellows were bound together in an uneasy truce. During one of their rare conversations he had explained that he was a photographer, but he never showed her any of his work. He spent hours of each day in the studio where he had discovered her. He said that he was working. She didn't understand how he could be. Sometimes she imagined that he only shut himself in there to get away from her. Once she had knocked on the door to bring him a letter she'd found on the mat. He had been lying on the sofa with his feet up and had not been pleased to be disturbed. She had not done it again. The rest of the day he spent in his garden and that did not seem like "work" either. He didn't grow anything useful. There were neither fruit trees nor rows of greens or other vegetables: just a tangled profusion of flowers that he didn't seem to be interested in straightening out. She had tried to help him with that and had pulled out weeds, which had been such a nuisance in her grandfather's garden. He hadn't said anything, but later, when she looked out of the kitchen window, she had seen him planting some of them back in.

Each evening she planned to leave early the next morning, before he was up, but somehow she always slept too long and it was then too late. She had never imagined that being "safe" would be like this. In the endless, dull days of the siege, when there had been no school and no warmth, not enough light and never sufficient to eat and only fear to vary the boredom, she had imagined life without war. Each day would have been filled with the things that she had missed so much. They would have piled up in her hands and overflowed like plump, ripe fruit. She would have bitten into them and laid their warm skins against her cheeks. Yet now she had no appetite. She longed to sleep and dream of happy times but the things she saw in the night left her choking with fear.

Then, one night, she dreamed of Alexander. She was watching him from so far away and though his features were indistinct, she knew, with the certainty of dreams, that the tiny figure on the hillside was him. He was standing apart from others, behind a barbed-wire fence. His ribs showed like scars and his neck and back were bent and pitiful. She was scrambling down the hillside from above, desperate to reach him, and she expected him to hold his hands out to her as he had when she was little. She expected him, despite all, to pick her up and swing her round but he didn't. She tried to call out to him but he was looking beyond her to someone who stood higher up. She turned round quickly, almost losing her footing on the slippery grass, but there was no one that she could see and when she turned back to speak to Alexander, he was gone too.

Her sense of disappointment and loss when she woke was too strong. When Paul asked, "And how are you?" she didn't give her newly learned reply of "Fine, thanks. And you?" Absentmindedly it slipped out.

"I dream of Alexander," she said.

"Alexander?" Paul Fellows had spilled his coffee.

"Yes. Alexander he is my biggest brother. I told you. He's twenty-seven, and I dream—"

"He's twenty-eight now."

"No! He isn't. I *know* this: he's *my* brother and I know. He's in the army. And—"

"Is he . . . really . . . in the army?" Paul Fellows asked hesitantly.

"Of course," Nina snapped. Didn't he understand that everybody was in the army? Even when men somehow kept on with their jobs they were always being called back to do a bit more fighting. Nick and Peter Gold had known about the war and cared; this man was so ignorant. Now he got up and went out to the studio without saying anything. He came back carrying a small handful of photographs, which he laid out on the table before her as if about to play solitaire.

"You take *my* picture!" Nina could barely speak. There was *her* photo of Alexander. "You steal it!"

"No."

"Yes!" She couldn't believe that he had done this and ran upstairs and snatched the envelope from the jacket pocket where she kept it.

He hadn't touched her photo. When she came downstairs again he didn't glance up.

"Paul?"

He wasn't even looking at the photos, but had his face buried in his hands. She took the two prints to the door and compared them in the unshadowed light.

"It isn't Alexander," she said, not really aware of why she spoke, only of her heart beating very fast.

"No."

"It's *you*, isn't it? It's *you* in Dubrovnik, with my mother."

"Yes."

Nina was scowling against the sun, trying to see the face of the young woman in the photo more clearly, forcing herself to understand.

"Yes," he went on, "that's me. That was taken in Dubrovnik when I was a young man. That was when I met Vera, your mother. I was there for the summer, studying art and architecture, and Dubrovnik was the most wonderful place I had ever seen. It was like magic. And your mother was . . ." He struggled for the word. But Nina had already gone.

She ran out of the house and garden and down the lane, stumbling in clumsy, borrowed shoes. She couldn't bear to hear him say it, to tell her that Alexander was his son. Was her brother Alexander, whom she had always loved so much, to be taken from her too?

13

TIED WITH A DOUBLE BOW

THE MUDDY RIVERBANK had dried up and cracked like a fragment of old, stained china. Nina scrambled down to get as near to the water as possible. She sat on a patch of grass among the flotsam of stranded sticks and swans' feathers and empty crab shells which were still as delicate and pink as any blossom. She picked one up, balancing it for a moment on the tip of her finger. When she blew softly it floated off and spun away into the river again.

Leaning over to follow its progress, she noticed the shadows of her own reflection; yet this was not what she wanted. She wanted to see a young woman's face, straight-browed against the sun. She longed for it to stare back at her, evenly and cheerfully. It wasn't there, and after all, she had never resembled her mother, neither in appearance nor character. Nina was the image of her rebellious grandmother, who had died so young.

Everyone agreed about that. Vera had been quieter, more patient, and utterly steadfast.

So how could her mother have betrayed them all like that? It was intolerable. And had the others known? Her brothers? Alexander himself? And what of her father? It was unbearable. How could her parents have lived this lie year after year, letting her think that everything in their lives was all right, when clearly, secretly, it must have been all wrong?

Yet their lives hadn't been like that. They had been happy, hadn't they? When the local militia had taken her father away the light in her mother's face had been taken too. Vera had continued caring for them through all the gray days of the siege, but her hair had turned white overnight, exactly as it did in her missing husband's fairy stories. Those stories had always told of innocent people stolen away, who never came back and whose families waited in vain for their return. Her mother had done that too, starting in hope at every footstep on the stairs. Sometimes as they sheltered in the cellars during a bombardment, Nina had listened to her mother and other adults talking bitterly of the war. When they spoke of shallow graves on silent farmland where wolves went at night, Nina always remembered the tales of enchanted caves deep in the forests where dragons and hideous sorcerers practiced their wickedness.

She remembered how her father used to come home from the university at the end of each day. He would open the door and blink with surprise and pleasure at the sight and sound of them all. He would push his glasses back up his nose and smile as they argued and teased and made plans about who could borrow his car that evening. It was as if, in the fairy-tale kingdoms of princes and plowmen, where young men rode magic foxes across the sky and rescued girls imprisoned in high towers, he temporarily forgot that there was this other family of flesh and blood, at home. Georg Topič had been older than her mother and the accepted family wisdom was that as a bookish, rather impractical man, he had been amazingly lucky to marry a woman like Vera. Her mother had never agreed with this opinion, insisting that she was the lucky one. But could they not both have been lucky?

Until the war began Nina had barely known a day of hardship. Her greatest worry had been that she might miss a film that other classmates got to see or that she wouldn't be invited to a friend's birthday party. There had been quarrels at home, of course there had, and they had been noisy and painful, with people slamming doors and stamping out, but her family had still been happy, hadn't it? Her mother had been so bossy, telling them all what to do and when to do it, and Nina had complained as much as anyone—more, probably. But it hadn't stopped any of them from being happy. Now that she knew her mother's secret she could not understand how their lives had been so pleasant and peaceful. She felt as though she had been tricked.

She had never imagined that her mother could have had any other life. This ordinary, middle-aged woman who was so ruthless in matters of honor and honesty, who would call anyone a liar to their face but not behind their back, and who had always defended them all, even Fahro, or especially Fahro, this quiet woman, her own mother, had, it seemed, been loved by somebody else, a stranger, from a foreign land and long ago.

And abandoned. There was no other explanation. And now

she, Nina, like the fairy-story beggar at the castle door, had asked for help from the same monster who had deserted a young woman and a baby! It was a wicked thing to do and she decided that Paul Fellows must have been a cold and selfish man who had never truly loved her mother. It was hardly surprising, therefore, that he didn't like *her* very much. There were no signs of another wife and children. He probably didn't like anyone very much.

Yet one thing continued to puzzle her: how had this secret lain hidden in that green box for all those long and happy years? How had she and Anja played their games beside it and never, ever suspected its existence?

"Hey!" A shout disturbed her.

She looked up but didn't answer. It was a boy about her own age.

"Hey! I thought I recognized them!" He dropped his bike on the grass and came down the bank toward her, pointing at something.

"I'm David," he said. She didn't answer but pulled a face and kicked a stick into the water. It spun round slowly. Maybe he'd take the hint and go.

"I'm David," he insisted, as though she should have been interested. "David Adams: *you* know!"

She shrugged, then understood. She was wearing *his* clothes, his castoffs! She knew that her face was bright red. His name was on those labels.

"I'm Gwen Adams's grandson." He was blushing too. "She's Paul's neighbor, so he came to us when you arrived. You've met my grandmother?"

She shook her head.

"No? Don't you remember her putting you to bed the day you arrived? No? Oh well, you'll see her again soon. She's longing to meet you properly, but I think she wanted to give you time to settle in. She lives in the cottage opposite Downlands and I spend lots of time with her, especially during holidays. We know your friend Paul very well. That's why he came to us right away for clothes for you. I've got loads more, if you need them. Or anything."

"I don't need your clothes."

"Oh."

"And Paul Fellows is *not* my friend."

"Really?" He stared at her in surprise, then threw another stick into the water, farther out than hers.

"Look!" She hadn't meant to cry out.

"What?"

She pointed, unable to explain. The two sticks appeared to be moving in opposite directions, as if this river could flow both ways. It made her feel suddenly desperate and she wondered again if she was imagining things. Was she going mad, like Fahro? Was she beginning to see things which weren't really there?

"It's just the current." He laughed.

She didn't understand so he settled down beside her and carefully explained that they were quite near the sea and that the river was tidal. At high tide water ran inland from the sea at the same time as the river water was still flowing out. Sometimes this river actually flowed both ways.

"It is true?" she asked, and when he nodded she almost smiled. It was the first time that someone had explained something to her in English and she had understood them.

"Well," he said, "I've got to go. My grandmother's waiting." He went back to his bike and waved as he cycled toward Southease, leaving her to watch the contrary flow of the river, and to remember that once upon a time in a faraway land, her grandfather had waited for her . . .

She was glad David had gone. She would not have liked him to see her sniff and wipe her eyes. Still, perhaps she had been rather rude about the clothes. It was absurd; all her life she'd grumbled about having to wear her brothers' old things and now it had happened again. She wished she could have explained that to him but she didn't regret what she'd said about Paul Fellows. He wasn't a friend at all.

And yet?

Once upon a time in a faraway land, someone had hidden a packet of letters in a faded green box at the very top of a house on a steep mountainside . . .

She remembered now: the box had been fastened with string tied in a double bow. With close, unwanted vividness she saw the attic again. She remembered how she and Anja, as little girls, had opened up the pale green box, teasing apart the rustling tissue paper and touching the rough cloth of the jacket within. Then, guiltily and regretfully, they had closed the lid and retied the string, struggling with the double bow. A double bow: she had never thought clearly about it before. That was what her grandfather always did. He tied everything securely with a neat double bow. It was as distinctive as a signature.

He alone had packed that box up, settling all the memories within so that they would be safe, not forgotten. She pictured him doing it, working quickly and methodically as he always did, folding up his wife's jacket, putting into it this part of his daughter-in-law's life so that it might be there for when it was needed. Maybe it hadn't been a secret at all. Maybe it was just that she, as a little girl, had been concerned with childish things and had never noticed it.

But the evidence was there: now that she knew the truth, she could see that it had been there all along and that she had loved the very things that had made Alexander special. This tall, angular Englishman with his untidy gray hair which had once been fair, and with his strong hands, was so clearly the father of her favorite brother. They even moved in the same way: she remembered her brother's long reach as he caught her, then cradled her in his arms. Wasn't that what she had seen when Paul Fellows reached down for the little cat?

Her grandfather had known all this. He had loved his daughter-in-law, this young woman from the south, who had left her own home and people in Dubrovnik and made a new home with them in Sarajevo. Yet others would not have been so kind. She suddenly realized what her mother must have suffered, how people must have pointed her out in the street, and gossiped behind her back. She knew exactly what they would have said: "Just look at her!" they'd have hissed unpleasantly. And to her face some would have said, "Stupid, that's what you are. Miss High-and-Mighty!" When her mother had said that she was going north to a new life in Sarajevo, some of her old neighbors would have snarled, "But I'll tell you something else: don't you ever try and come back! Because I won't help you again, you dirty little slut. I won't even open the door." And on the other side of the road somebody would have stopped to stare before he resumed his brief walk home.

But not her grandfather. Never. Why, on the last day at the bottom of the stairs he'd struggled to tie that double bow again. He had wanted to tie up what was left over from their former life and he had sent her out to live, for all of them, what was yet to come.

And she'd gone. Now she got to her feet restlessly and irritably. How could she have done that? The two sticks had been carried so far apart by the currents that they would never meet and she had almost lost sight of them, so she turned away. There was nothing else to do down here. She might as well go back.

Slowly, she retraced her steps, still wondering how she could have left them all like that. How could she have picked up her bag and walked away from her grandfather, knowing that she was not going to see him again, as though she didn't care at all? Why, she hadn't even written the letter, when that was all that he had asked of her. Just a letter.

She came round the side of the house silently so that no one would know. Outside the open kitchen door she stopped. Paul was talking to someone inside. A woman answered him. Her reply mentioned Nina's name but was too quiet for her to catch. Guiltily, she slid onto the bench outside the door, drew her legs up so that no one might see her shadow, and settled down among the droning bees and the erratic sideways flight of butterflies, to try to overhear.

"Of course," Paul was saying, "she's not really like her mother, not in looks, but there is something. The very first time I saw her down by the river, I noticed something. I couldn't ignore her: there was something about her and if she hadn't looked so angry I would, I suppose, have asked if I could take her picture. She had—has—such an expression, but it's not her mother's. Then, when she turned up in the studio and with those letters, too, that I'd written nearly thirty years ago, I was *so* shocked, Gwen."

"Not as shocked as she must have been!" the woman remarked sharply. "Really, Paul," she continued, "I'd always thought we were friends. And now I learn that you have a grown-up son somewhere, whom you've never ever seen! How could you do that?"

"I wanted to see him. I've thought about him. But somehow I never got round to it."

"Really, Paul! 'Never got round to it.' You make it sound like painting the house."

"I know," he said. "I know. You're right. And now it's probably too late."

"Too late?" The woman's voice was gentle, and Nina wished that she had not hidden herself away. She would have liked to meet David's grandmother.

"Yes. What with the war. When it started I asked to be sent out there as one of the war photographers, but all the papers said no. And they were right in a way. I am too old. After the Falklands, which was the last war I covered, I decided that I never wanted to see such things again, and when I saw the pictures from the Gulf, I knew that I was right. I was past all that. War reporting is a young man's game. At least that's what I told myself until I heard about fighting in the former Yugoslavia. I knew then that my son was there, somewhere. I went to all the papers, all the agencies, and begged to be sent, offered to pay all my own expenses, but they all said no. Nicely, of course, but the message was clear: you are too old now, Paul. And do you know, each time I heard it, I became more and more angry."

"Why?"

"Why? Haven't you seen the pictures in the papers? Haven't you watched the television news?"

"I don't understand."

"Because war is about killing *young* men! It is about old men like me sending young men, who are barely more than boys, out to kill and be killed. Suddenly I found that I was 'too old' so must be kept safe, whereas my son, my only child, was just the right age to die—"

"No!" Nina shouted, bursting in from her hiding place. "Don't say that!"

He tried to explain, but she couldn't or wouldn't understand and she hated him again. How could anyone say that there was a "right age to die"? How could anyone be so stupid?

If she had been able to, she would have described the pictures that lived more vividly in her mind than any photograph on any page. She could have told him about Fahro and her grandfather, about the little boy lost along the road at dusk, and the women and children waiting in the lines for water and for bread, but she didn't. She looked scornfully at this cold, unloving man and was not able to say anything at all.

"Paul didn't mean that—" Gwen Adams tried to explain, but Nina wouldn't listen and went up to her room and banged the door shut.

14

TALKING TO FRIENDS

SUMMER HOVERED, then settled over Downlands and Southease and the river beyond. It was hot and Nina, who had heard only of English rain, was surprised. An uneasy cease-fire had been negotiated between her and Paul Fellows. They were cautious of each other and avoided talking about either the war or Alexander. She knew she should be grateful that he had taken her in and she was. He had helped her to apply for political asylum and registered her with the Red Cross. He was often on the phone with them, having hushed conversations that he seemed to be hiding from Nina. He was doing everything that he could. She knew that. He was even arranging for her to attend school when the summer holidays were over and she was pleased, but she did not like him any better and sometimes hated herself for that too. Gwen Adams tried to help. She came over often and explained that Paul had no family of his own: he knew almost nothing of children.

"But I'm *not* a child!" Nina protested angrily and Gwen shook her head and shrugged and gave up.

Some days went really well. Others were misery. After Nina had been there several weeks Paul took her out to buy some "proper" clothes. He had promised this shopping trip ages ago and she had been so excited. She reminded him about it several times a day. On the morning that it was finally arranged she awoke as full of expectations as if it had been New Year's Eve or even her own birthday, which had always been a big celebration at home. Paul had groaned when she asked yet again what time they were leaving.

She wanted to go at once. She wanted to spend the whole day browsing around the brightly lit shops. She thought she would enjoy it now: she understood the money and a lot of what people said. She wanted to shop all day and stagger home in the evening with armfuls of brand-new shopping bags. Shopping was what everyone did abroad. She knew that from friends and relatives who had been to Europe and America before the war. She had seen it on the television. She too would stroll up and down the clean, safe streets, without a care in the world and have things that she wanted.

It did not seem greedy; in fact, it did not seem much to ask, after all that had happened. She wanted to start again, to get beyond the grasp of what lay in the past and she could not do that while she was still wearing jeans with some strange boy's name stitched in the back.

That morning Paul got up late. She watched impatiently as the clock moved steadily to ten. She nearly died of impatience. Then he said he had work to do: they couldn't leave until the afternoon. She could have screamed. He was so selfish! She still didn't believe that he really worked in that studio. Whenever she peeped in he was stretched out on the sofa reading, or was just sitting, staring at nothing. If he'd cared about her, he'd have been proud to take her out to the shops; he'd have wanted her to look nice; he'd have demonstrated that she was more important than a load of photographs.

The trip was not a success. At first it had seemed simple. They had driven to a large, busy town and begun to walk around. She had spotted clothes in a window at once, long before he did, and insisted that they go in and look. She picked things out eagerly: jeans, T-shirts, a sweater, underclothes, and a nylon jacket with a furry collar. She was pleased. Then Nina looked around her. The things she had chosen appeared childish somehow. She put them back and picked up others. No, he said, these were not her size; no, those were all wrong, too cheap, then too expensive. It was confusing. The shops were overheated and smelled strongly of something that wasn't quite perfume. They went somewhere else, which was definitely more fashionable. She picked up everything, unable to make up her mind.

Paul tried to help. He held a checked shirt under her chin.

"No!" she cried, exasperated. "No! I don't like." How could he ever have thought that a red like that would look nice on her? He turned away and sat down on a chair, tapping the arm with a gesture of impatience. She knew that she was behaving badly, but she couldn't stop.

Then she saw a display of pale, silky sweaters: pinks and lilacs and the softest greens and blues. She took two and then another. They were just the sort of thing she had always loved.

He held up a finger to indicate that she could only take one, so she flung them all down, unable to believe that he could be so mean. In the end they bought almost nothing, just socks and pajamas that she knew were too small.

They drove home in total silence and she kept her face turned away so that he wouldn't see her tears of disappointment and guilt. She was amazed that she had behaved like that. Her mother would have been so ashamed of her; indeed, she hardly recognized herself at all.

A nice girl, like Anja, would never have been as ungrateful as that.

It was fortunate, then, that the good weather held. She was able to spend time out of the house and away from Paul. People from the tiny cluster of houses began to recognize her and to smile. Nobody stopped to talk, but she supposed that this was the English way. Even David was not much of a talker. He spent a lot of time fishing on the river and sometimes they sat together watching the uncertain progress of the float. He never caught anything, but he didn't mind, and Nina was surprised to find that she enjoyed just sitting there in silence, trying to work out the mysteries of this river which flowed both ways.

David was almost exactly the same age as she was but was interested in things that she knew nothing of. He knew about birds and plants and wild animals and wanted to study something called ecology. When she asked what that was he said that it was "nature." He showed her where swans had nested on a promontory farther down the river and one warm summer evening they startled two herons among a patch of reeds. They watched the pair fly to the far bank, where they circled once, then twice, then seemed to change their minds because they glided away with the evening sun dyeing their silver necks red. He'd even seen badgers at the foot of the hills, he said proudly. She tried hard to be impressed because she realized it was important to him but she couldn't imagine what a badger could possibly be like.

Often he infuriated her. He knew so much about this small area of the country but had no idea where Bosnia was. Then she was tempted to treat him like some stupid little boy who didn't understand anything about the real world. At other times she was jealous. She'd watch from her bedroom window. He'd leave his grandmother's cottage, unchain his bike from her fence, and cycle casually away to his home. At the corner of the green he always turned around to wave to Gwen. He'd let go of the handlebars completely when he waved, like a real show-off. Then he'd stand up on the pedals and pound over the uphill bit to get to the main road. Gwen remained in her garden watching affectionately until her grandson was out of sight and Nina envied them both. Sometimes she secretly hoped he'd lose his balance and fall off, but he never did.

David was not the only one who was ignorant. Nina could not believe how little Paul and Gwen knew about Yugoslavian history. One evening when they were all together she brought down her grandmother's jacket to show them.

"See?" she cried proudly. Certainly it fit much better, now that she was not so thin.

When they looked puzzled, as though they did not understand the significance of the uniform, or of that earlier war, she began to explain excitedly. She had never realized until now that people in other parts of the world knew so little about the history of the country that had been Yugoslavia. To her it had always been the center of the world. To them it was only a very distant place. She told them some of the stories that her grandfather had told her: of how he and his young wife had fought with Tito against the Fascists and the invading Nazis during the Second World War. She told them about the birth of her father in a cave in the mountains and of how his mother had carried him on her back through the forests. They said that it sounded like a fairy tale and she was irritated because she thought they were not taking her seriously.

All this time, through these hot summer days, and nights when darkness never came and she could not fall asleep, she was tormented by the letter that she could not write. She had tried several times but could not bear the thought of writing a letter that might never be opened or read, and might not even be delivered. Though she now accepted that her grandfather must be dead, she still clung to the hope that Alexander might be alive.

She imagined her letter left lying at the bottom of some sack of unclaimed mail not just for weeks, but for months which stretched into years. Sometimes, as she lay on her bed through the hot afternoons, she imagined their house in the mountains, abandoned now to neglect and the raging summer sun. The paint would blister and crack and the shutters would swing and swing and when autumn came with its winds, they would finally tear free. By then the lilac at the gate would have withered and died because nobody would have carried out a single jug of water all summer long. In the orchards the trees would have bloomed unseen and the cherries would have ripened and softened. Their bright skin would have split open and the bruised flesh would have turned brown among the overgrown weeds at the foot of the trees.

If anyone still went up those mountain paths, the letter with her neat, clear writing on the envelope would be pushed under the door and then lie there forever and ever. She could not bear to write and ask questions that might never be answered, so she did nothing at all. All summer long, while the honeysuckle and the rambling roses bloomed over the walls of Southease, she trailed this ignorance behind her like an ugly, broken wing which she could not tear off.

She was restless and could not stay in one place for long. She began a dozen tasks around the house but left them all uncompleted.

Then one hot afternoon when blackened storm clouds raced across the Downs and the last light before coming rain lay as heavy as a pool of spilled honey, she picked a quarrel with Paul Fellows. It was about nothing at all. He had asked her to take the washing in. She had said she would, but hadn't. He'd asked her again and she'd sighed. Then he said crossly:

"For heaven's sake, Nina, can't you ever do anything to help?"

Grudgingly she dragged the plastic basket from its place and then hesitated at the door. Fat drops of rain were already falling, releasing the smell of sun from the dry earth and the dusty step. He snatched the basket from her and did the task himself, dropping things in his haste, and coming in finally with his shirt wet through and the clothes dreadfully tangled.

"You make a mess," she tried to joke and would have sorted it out, from the safety of the kitchen, if he hadn't kicked the door shut so violently that it rattled the mugs on their hooks.

"Didn't your mother teach you anything?" He did not disguise his disapproval. "For crying out loud, Nina, you really are a lazy little—"

"I am *not* lazy!"

"But you are! Look at you! You haven't done a thing for days!" He was separating her clothes from his, pulling the things apart. "They really must have spoiled you, the only girl among so many brothers. And I'm surprised. It wasn't like that when I was there. It was the opposite, if anything. Women did so much. That was what I liked about your mother—she was so lively, so energetic. A remarkable girl, your mother was."

"Don't speak of my mother like that. You have no right. You never cared about her. If you had loved her you would never have left her alone like that!"

She was screaming at him.

"You didn't love her and you don't love my brother! You don't want any of us!"

"I do."

"You *don't*. You didn't come for her. You didn't help her!" She was as furious as if she were the young woman abandoned to her fate. "You didn't want them!"

"I did. I wanted them both. It was your mother, Vera, who didn't want me."

She was too furious to understand. Outside the rain fell even more heavily.

"She was coming here, Nina, she was coming here to this

house and to me. Then she changed her mind. I had sent them two tickets, one for your mother and one for Alexander. Everything was waiting for them and I waited and waited. But they didn't come."

"I don't believe you." She ran from the house and up to the main road and when a bus came by a few minutes later she climbed onboard and went into the little town; because of the rain, people smiled to see her so soaked through and nobody suspected that she was crying.

She went into the pharmacy to kill time and to keep out of the rain. She tried out lipsticks and perfume until there was no room left on her wrists.

There had been plane tickets. She remembered them clearly. Nick and Peter Gold had been intrigued by them and had examined them in great detail in Trieste. So that was why. They had pointed out the dates, but she had not understood why they were so intrigued and they had not questioned her. It hurt her to admit that Paul hadn't been lying. He had sent Vera two plane tickets to fly to England, but for reasons that they would now never know her mother had decided not to come.

Nina had spent so long in the shop that she sensed that people had noticed her. She glanced around for something to buy and then remembered. She had just enough money for a small bottle of peroxide. When she had bought it she realized that she had no money left for the bus fare home. It was a long walk and the light was fading by the time she reached the bridge.

"Nina! Ni–na!" At first she thought she was imagining it, but in the end, she recognized Paul's voice. She was surprised and pleased that he had bothered to look for her. Then she saw him running toward her.

His shoes and jeans were covered with streaks of gray mud and she suddenly understood that he had been worried about her, and was annoyed with her for not saying where she was going. When he reached out and pulled her toward him she didn't turn away, but mumbled that she was sorry. Then they walked back to the house arm in arm.

Three days later, when he was away in London taking pictures for a magazine, she bleached her hair. It didn't go quite right. When David came around to see if she wanted to come fishing, his jaw dropped. He said her hair looked "different." Gwen laughed out loud and said she'd better borrow a hat. She did and thought she looked quite smart, really, almost arty. David kept his eyes firmly on the floor. When Paul came back that evening he was furious with her. He said that she looked an absolute sight. What did she think she was doing, ruining her hair like that?

"It's *my* hair . . ." she began angrily and was just about to tell him that it was nothing to do with him when the telephone rang. He picked it up at once, but the line went dead.

And then she smiled at him; suddenly, and from nowhere at all, came the realization that she didn't mind him going on about her ridiculous hair. It was what they would have done at home.

Later that night the phone rang repeatedly. Nina turned over and heard Paul going downstairs. Then he called her. He was holding the phone out to her, unable to say anything at all. She listened, and heard, but couldn't speak either. The voice on the other end was asking for "Nina, Nina Topič?"

"Yes?"

"It's me, it's Alexander. Is that you, Nina?"

She nodded, with tears running down her face so fast that she could only sniff.

"I'm in Belgrade, Nina. I've just seen your name on a Red Cross list . . . Nina?"

She put the phone into Paul's hand and then stood very close, leaning her head of bright, bleached hair against his shoulder as, slowly and hesitantly, he began to talk. And while she listened, he stretched his arm around her shoulder and held her there, close, and she didn't mind at all.